ROMEO & JULIET & *Vampires*

ROMEO & JULIET & Vampires

ADAPTED FROM
WILLIAM SHAKESPEARE
BY CLAUDIA GABEL

HARPER TEEN
An Imprint of HarperCollinsPublishers

HarperTeen is an imprint of HarperCollins Publishers.

Romeo & Juliet & Vampires
Adaptation copyright © 2010 by Claudia Gabel
www.harperteen.com
Library of Congress Cataloging-in-Publication Data is available.
ISBN 978-0-06-197624-7
Typography by Ray Shappell
10 11 12 13 14   CG/RRDH   10 9 8 7 6 5 4 3 2 1
❖
First Edition

PROLOGUE

TRANSYLVANIA, 1462

or the past six years, the Wallachian Province of Transylvania was ruled by Vlad the Impaler, a ruthless prince responsible for the deaths of forty thousand European people during his reign. Vladimir couldn't have accomplished this horrific feat alone, of course. A special part of his constituency—a family of vampires known as the Capulets—helped him carry out this murderous rampage by feeding off of "undesirables" one by one.

In exchange for their "work," the Capulets were given a large, imposing castle in the southern part of the Carpathian Mountains near the city of Transylvania and anything else their hearts desired. They enjoyed the benefits of being wealthy aristocrats by day, bloodsuckers by night—opulent clothes; priceless jewels;

supernatural powers; and immortality. They owned most of the land in the area and had servants to tend to their every whim.

One might say that to be a Capulet was to be both envied and abhorred. However, if you were talking with a Montague, he would have told you that the Capulets were mercenaries of evil who had to be destroyed.

Blessed with a keen sense of intuition and vampire-slaying skills that could not be matched, the Montagues fought the Capulets at every opportunity to keep them from terrorizing the citizens of Transylvania. Their hope was to rid the world of these beasts, once and for all.

But recently the rules of war were changed. Prince Vladimir was ousted from the throne and imprisoned, leaving his half brother Radu in power. Radu's first act as prince was to institute a peace treaty in the region of Wallachia, thereby forcing the Montagues and the Capulets into a truce.

But could peace really exist between sworn enemies, especially when one was as bloodthirsty as the Capulet family?

From forth the fatal loins of these two foes, a pair of star-cross'd lovers were fated to find out.

Citizens of Transylvania,

With Vlad the Impaler imprisoned for his crimes against humanity, the era of his violence is officially over. A peace treaty has been reached between the new government and Vladimir's mercenaries, the Capulets.

If any humans or vampires commit a violent act that results in the injury or death of another, their lives shall pay the forfeit of the peace.

Abiding by this simple, yet definitive law should lead to civility and tranquillity in our kingdom.

—Prince Radu

CHAPTER ONE

Juliet sat on her bed and stared at her reflection in an ornate gilded mirror, which she held close to her face. With her fingertip, she traced the outline of her rose-hued lips on the glass, repeating the same movement over the subtle slope of her nose and the smooth youthful brow above her indigo-colored eyes.

She was not one to be vain. But in three days, the simple act of checking to see if a chestnut-colored tendril had fallen loose from one of her hair combs would not be so simple. Truth be told, it wouldn't even be possible, for Juliet's reflection would cease to exist.

"Keep your chin up, my lady," said a voice from behind her. "God knows it will improve your posture."

Juliet felt her breath catch in her throat, surprised to hear that someone else was in her chambers. She set the mirror down on her lap and turned toward the door, where her beloved nursemaid stood, dressed in a white smock and holding a wooden brush in her hand.

Juliet sighed. Her nurse was here to help her prepare for a lavish ball that her parents were hosting this evening. However, Juliet would rather hide in her chambers for the night than play the role of dutiful daughter in a room full of vampires and strangers—especially since she was in such a somber mood.

"I have more important things to be concerned about than my posture," Juliet said as she rose from her bed, still clutching the ivory handle of her mirror.

She walked over to the leaded terrace window and gazed at the snowcapped mountains that lined the far reaches of Transylvania. As a child, she'd dreamed of leaving the castle and disappearing into the hills, where she'd befriend all the wild animals and live off of berries. How foolish she had been.

"I suppose you are referring to your birthday." The nurse strode across the room, her short, meaty legs pounding the marble floor. She stood behind Juliet and removed her mistress's robe, quickly pulling it off of both her arms. "Most girls look forward to turning sixteen. Or am I mistaken?"

Juliet closed her eyes, feeling the last ray of the setting sun tickle her skin through her thin cotton slip. Soon, exposure to direct sunlight would be the kiss of death for her.

"Most girls do not have to kill someone and drink every last drop of their blood in order to live a day past it," she said.

The nurse circled in front of Juliet and glowered at her. "Well, there's no sense in wishing for what is unattainable. Now sit back down so I can untangle that nest of hair before Lady Capulet comes to call. We cannot have her seeing you so unkempt."

Juliet nodded and shuffled over to her bed, heeding the nurse's command. She knew better than anyone how easy it was to be scared of Lady Capulet.

But there was one thing more frightening than the matriarch of the Capulet family: a surprise raid on the castle by the vampire-slaying Montagues. There had been three security breaches before—guerrilla attacks in retaliation for the brutal murders the Capulets had carried out at the hands of Vlad the Impaler.

In those dire hours, Juliet had always been fiercely protected, mostly by her older cousin Tybalt. But now she couldn't help but wonder if she would've been better off as a casualty. Of course, being dead would free her from her troubles, but dying at the hands of the Montagues would only cause more destruction in Transylvania. The Capulets hated the Montagues with every fiber of their unbeating hearts, and would certainly seek vengeance at any cost. She couldn't bear the thought of being responsible for *anyone's* death, regardless of who they were.

Juliet let out a deep breath and tried to force these disconcerting thoughts from her mind. As the hairbrush's soft bristles massaged her scalp, she recalled a more carefree time, when she used to love counting the brushstrokes and listening to her nurse sing happy folk songs while she worked. When the nurse's own child died many years ago, she practically adopted Juliet, and Juliet felt she could trust her nurse with anything.

"Don't you take any pity on me, Nurse?" she asked, her voice despondent and desperate for sympathy. "Or my soon-to-be-damned soul?"

Juliet heard no response as the brush kept moving through her hair. But then there was a pause, and Juliet felt the nurse's lips press down on the crown of her head.

"I do, child," the nurse replied tenderly. "When you have doubts, remember that I've been preparing my heart for this since you were born. It's been a wretched task."

A tear trickled down Juliet's cheek, which she quickly wiped away. "Thank you, I will."

The nurse wrapped her arms around Juliet and squeezed. "Is there anything I can do to cheer you up?"

"Yes, switch lives with me," Juliet said with a small grin.

The nurse laughed into Juliet's ear. "That is quite a favor to ask."

"I know, but you cannot blame me for trying," Juliet replied, her eyes smiling just a little.

Suddenly there was a knock at the chamber door and the nurse snapped to attention.

"I wasn't expecting her ladyship for another hour or so," she gasped. The nurse handed Juliet the brush, then raced over to the closet and opened it.

Juliet managed a girlish giggle. Unlike the other vampires who slept until nightfall, Lady Capulet's eyes always popped open the moment twilight arrived. "Well, my mother does love to keep her human underlings on their toes."

The nurse fetched Juliet's robe, shaking her head with disapproval. "Nobody likes a young maiden with a sharp tongue."

"I suppose it will go well with my new sharp teeth."

Another knock sounded at the door—loud and demanding.

"Just mind yourself, *please*," the nurse advised Juliet.

"Why should I? I have only a few days left of being human. I might as well enjoy myself," she replied.

"Good heavens. Maybe you should keep your mouth shut altogether," the nurse said as she smoothed back Juliet's hair and tied it at the nape of her neck with a black satin ribbon. Then she took a deep breath, walked hastily toward the door, and opened it.

At the sight of Lady Capulet, Juliet shuddered as

though a gust of wind had blown by. The nurse bowed her head respectfully and said, "My lady."

Without a word or acknowledgment of her daughter's servant, Lady Capulet floated into the bedchamber, her dainty feet hovering a good six inches off the ground. She was dressed in a long ebony gown, and folded her hands delicately in front of her chest as she gracefully levitated across the room. Her pale yellow skin was utterly flawless and her raven-colored hair was pulled back tightly in an ornate bun so that her glowing red irises were impossible to ignore.

There were no vampires more beautiful, nor imposing, than Lady Capulet. Juliet could barely blink in her mother's presence—she was that captivating—and until today, Juliet hadn't noticed their resemblance. With her transition from human to vampire to come in three days, there was no way she could deny it now.

"Nurse, leave us. I must speak with my daughter in private," Lady Capulet said firmly.

Juliet's heart fluttered with dismay. She did not want to lose the support of her most precious ally.

"As you wish," the nurse replied, bowing her head again and closing the door behind her.

Juliet swallowed hard, hoping something cheerful, like a chirping bird outside her window, would break the uncomfortable silence.

Lady Capulet glided over to the nightstand near Juliet's bed and held her hand over the top of a copper oil lamp. A flickering flame suddenly appeared, showering Juliet's face with a light golden sheen. While all female vampires had some degree of conjuring powers, Lady Capulet's skills were far above the rest.

"Come, let me see you," Lady Capulet said, staring deep into Juliet's eyes and running a long, sharp fingernail down her daughter's cheek.

Juliet willed herself not to shed any more tears. Lady Capulet did not tolerate babyish behavior.

"Your color is already beginning to change," Lady Capulet said with a proud expression on her face. "Can you tell?"

"I haven't thought to look, Mother," Juliet lied, and glanced away.

The first sign of transformation had begun last night—her healthy, pink skin tone was gradually turning pale. Soon her eyes would start to alter in color—from ice blue to glowing scarlet—and her fingernails would grow long and sharp. The ability to levitate and smell blood would follow, as well as the loss of her reflection and shadow.

But there was one symptom of the transition that was so excruciating, even a vampire as strong as her cousin Tybalt had difficulty handling it—a ravenous hunger that would gnaw mercilessly at her insides, until she performed her initiation rite before midnight on her sixteenth birthday.

The only way for Juliet to stop the transformation

was to refuse initiation, which she desperately wanted to do. The ritual was the final step to becoming a full-fledged vampire, and known only to those within the vampire community. Juliet would have to hunt down a human and kill him—all by herself, and without the help of any accomplice. Then she must ingest *every ounce* of her victim's blood until his corpse was nothing but a dry, shriveled shell. But as abhorrent as the initiation ritual was to Juliet, resisting it would lead to starvation and death. Juliet wasn't sure she had the stomach for that kind of intense suffering.

Lady Capulet quickly became stern, dropping her hand over the lamp's flame and extinguishing it. "Are you still trying to pretend that your destiny as a vampire does not await you? That will not do you any good."

"And what should I do?" The anger in Juliet's voice was unmistakable. "Embrace a fate that will rid me of my humanity and morality? A fate that will force me to feed off the blood of man, or else dig myself an early grave?"

"Juliet, your theatrics are both tiring and tedious," said Lady Capulet. "I transitioned on my sixteenth birthday without an ounce of reluctance. And so did your father, and his father before him. All your hand-wringing is a great disrespect to your lineage."

Juliet lay down on her bed, turning so that her back was to Lady Capulet. "At least we can agree on this—we are both ashamed of each other."

The room went eerily quiet and Juliet's stomach churned. She knew what she had said was horrible, but she was so eager to convince her mother that her family's lifestyle was, in a word, depraved. At this point, Juliet would say anything to make Lady Capulet realize that feeding on humans was wrong—even if that meant provoking a fight.

"*Shame?*" Lady Capulet's voice was loud enough to rattle all the glass in the room. Juliet covered her ears with her hands. "Are we not here, living in this splendid castle like royalty? Are we not the most powerful force in Transylvania, despite the cruel acts of lowly poachers like the Montagues?"

Juliet could feel herself coming undone, so she steeled herself and pretended her nurse was by her side.

"My aim is not to be ungrateful, Mother. It is to be truthful," Juliet said. "And the truth is that some see the Montagues as vigilantes, and think their actions are justified."

"Do you share the same sentiment?" Her mother's stare practically took Juliet's breath away.

"I do not know how you can live with the blood of thousands on your hands," Juliet replied after a moment of awkward silence.

"It is easy when you have orders to kill," Lady Capulet said, smoothing a few stray hairs back with her palms. "But now the peace treaty is threatening our human blood supply, which means we are more vulnerable than we have ever been before."

"Vulnerable or not, I don't think I can go through with the initiation. I am sorry to let you down, Mother," Juliet said.

Lady Capulet floated around Juliet's covered four-poster bed, then settled in a high-backed armchair so she could look Juliet in the eyes.

"Even in death, my child, you will be a member of the Capulet family." Juliet's mother extended her hand into the air and a brown paper envelope materialized above it. "So before you decide to starve yourself, why don't you carefully consider the alternatives?"

Juliet sat up slowly, reached above her head, and took the envelope in her hand. After loosening the wax seal on the back of it with her thumb, she began to read the wrinkled parchment that was enclosed as Lady Capulet floated out of the room and closed the door behind her.

Dear Juliet,

Your lord and ladyship have shared with me that soon you will become a full member of the vampire race. I would like to extend my heartfelt congratulations to you. All the special powers you have yet to possess will serve you well and you will take great joy in them. And though you feel conflicted about your initiation rite, I know you will eventually come to understand that immortality is a treasure worth killing for.

It must seem odd receiving such an intimate letter from a stranger, but I am pleased to inform you that I will be attending the Capulet ball. Some find my nature to be plain, but my reputation in our ranks is highly esteemed. In any case, I am very anxious to meet you.

With noble intentions,
Count Paris

Juliet crumpled up the letter and held it tightly in both her hands. She knew other maidens her age had received notes like this before and wound up married to strangers their parents had picked out for them.

Juliet's skin prickled with nervous chills just thinking of it, so she pulled the covers up to her chin, gripping the fabric tightly with her fingers. If her mother thought that a romance—especially one that was prearranged—would rid Juliet of her depression, she was sorely mistaken.

·

CHAPTER TWO

At the bottom of the steep, rocky hill upon which Capulet Castle was erected stood the Montague family arsenal. Built as large as a fortress with Gothic architecture as beautiful as any cathedral, no structure in Transylvania was as intimidating or awe-inspiring. With the dreaded Prince Vladimir now imprisoned for his heinous crimes, and Vlad's half brother Radu proclaiming this a new era of "peace," the Montagues had been ordered to close their arsenal.

However, despite Prince Radu's hope for harmony and order, the Montagues continued to store and maintain a considerable amount of weaponry—battle-axes, wooden pikes, broadswords, quarterstaffs, and the like—in case of a vampire crisis. Needless to say, most of the Montagues did not believe that the Capulets were capable of honoring a long-term truce. In their opinion, the vampires were an evil plague on humanity, and the only way to stop them was by stamping them out, one by one.

On the night of the Capulet ball, Romeo Montague—the youngest gentleman of the brood—sat in his family's drafty arsenal, sharpening his father's parrying daggers and misericorde knives with his older cousin Benvolio and his dear friend Mercutio. Romeo had been working on one knife for the last ten minutes, his sand-colored hair flopping over his brown eyes and his mind totally lost in a daydream. This is what set him apart from the rest of the Montagues—fighting vampires wasn't the only thing he thought about.

"If you do not keep your attention on your blade there, Romeo, you will have one less finger with which to tie your bootlaces," Benvolio said, grinning.

Romeo drew his gaze back from a dripping leak in one of the stone walls, returning it to the knife sharpener in his hands. "That would probably hurt less than this broken heart of mine."

Mercutio groaned as he examined a well-used crossbow. "My God, Romeo. Are you still lamenting over that grizzly beast Rosaline Capulet?"

Recently Romeo had become obsessed with a fair and lovely maiden named Rosaline. On several occasions, he had tried to talk to her, but she just ignored him. It had really hurt his feelings.

"Of course he is, Mercutio! Those half-breed females

are quite enticing," Benvolio said in reply. "I heard from Raulfe the blacksmith that they smell just like bacon."

Romeo slammed the knife and sharpener down on a worktable so that they made a loud clanging sound.

"You are two of the most ignorant bastards in Transylvania," he said.

"And handsome, too," Mercutio joked.

Romeo was unable to prevent himself from smirking. "The only one who thinks so is your mother."

"What are you implying? That my mother has bad taste?" Mercutio said, apparently offended.

"If you ask me, Romeo, you are the one whose taste is laughable," Benvolio added.

"Is that so?" Romeo could feel his pulse rising. He had a short temper when his cousin and friend made fun of him, which unfortunately was quite often.

"Yes, a half-breed Capulet is not worthy of anything but scorn and suspicion." Benvolio picked up a longsword and ran a gloved finger over the silver blade, making sure it was sharp.

"Rosaline is a human being, not a half-breed," Romeo stated firmly.

"Just for now," Mercutio corrected. "Next year at this time, she will become a vampire. And what will you do then? Watch as she eats live goats?"

Benvolio nudged Mercutio with a devilish grin on his round face. "Perhaps you are being too hasty with your criticism. Her wildness could do Romeo a great deal of service . . . especially in bed."

Mercutio slapped his leg as he laughed. "Honestly, Benvolio, I would be wary of dropping my trousers in front of my wife if she had fangs."

"And an uncontrollable appetite for blood," Benvolio said, chuckling.

A flood of anger ripped through Romeo's body. He made his hands into fists and brought them up to his face. "How about we settle this debate the old-fashioned way, Benvolio?"

Another chuckle erupted from Benvolio's belly. "You are barely sixteen and have not fought anyone in your life. I would crush you in seconds."

Romeo's older cousin spoke the truth. In his family's crusade against Vladimir's vampire army, Romeo had no kills, or even serious injuries, to his credit. Though his cousin teased him mercilessly about this, his parents thought he was still too young for combat. A part of Romeo was relieved to have been spared the ugliness of the war. He believed in protecting the villagers from anyone who would do them harm, but as he gaped at all the weaponry that surrounded him, he feared that his family was becoming more and more like the murderers they had vowed to stop.

Still, wasn't the honor of Rosaline's name worth taking a beating for? Besides, Romeo had learned excellent long-sword skills from his father, the master vampire slayer Lord Montague. Perhaps he could beat his cousin by using a few tricks he had been secretly perfecting. There was only one way to know.

"Hear this, Benvolio!" Romeo shouted, jumping onto the worktable and snatching a long-sword that was hanging on the wall. He aimed the pointed tip at his cousin and said, "Prepare for me to butcher you, you fat ugly cow!"

Benvolio and Mercutio looked at each other and burst into a riotous fit of laughter.

"Come down from there, Romeo. You're going to fall off that table, smack your head on the ground, and split your head open," Mercutio warned him.

"Let the cow fight his own battles, Mercutio," Romeo said.

"Have it your way, Cousin." Benvolio nodded his head at Mercutio, who quickly took a finely crafted long-sword out of a leather sheath and handed it to him. Benvolio went into a strong fighting stance and held the sword up with his right hand. "Let the thrashing of your life begin!"

Romeo narrowed his eyes at Benvolio as his cousin leaped onto the table. He immediately lunged forward, barely allowing Romeo any time to react. Romeo blocked Benvolio's strike with a mighty jab of his sword, and then swiftly shoved him with his left hand.

Benvolio stumbled back a few steps, almost falling off the edge of the table. When he regained his balance, he grinned.

"Nicely done," he said, impressed. "I did not know you had that in you."

"Oh, I am full of surprises," Romeo said.

Benvolio charged again, his sword aiming high at Romeo's head. Romeo ducked at the last moment and then swept his sword near Benvolio's feet, hoping to trip him up. Benvolio was too fast, though, blocking Romeo's sword with his own, all the while a smug look forming on his face.

"Come on, Romeo! Get him!" Mercutio called out from the corner of the room.

Benvolio swiped at Romeo two more times with his sword, which Romeo defended easily. "Why are you cheering for him and not me?"

"I always bet on the underdog!" Mercutio said.

Romeo saw that his opponent was distracted and whipped his sword at Benvolio's left arm. The tip of the blade cut a hole in Benvolio's shirt from his elbow to his shoulder.

"Damn you! This is one of my favorites!" Benvolio growled.

"I am not the least bit sorry," Romeo said.

"You will be in a moment," Benvolio said, swinging his sword at Romeo rapidly.

Romeo dodged three of Benvolio's swipes in a row. But then, Benvolio's shiny metal blade sliced down toward his legs, and Romeo spun out of the way just in time. He wasn't so lucky when Benvolio charged at him again—Romeo was forced off the worktable and hit the floor, face-first.

Romeo groaned in pain at the blunt impact, then slowly rolled over onto his back and touched his nose with the palm of his left hand. He craned his head up to see if there was blood on it, and sighed when he saw his guess was correct.

Out of breath and sweating profusely, Benvolio yanked the sword out of Romeo's grip, his playful mood suddenly turned serious. "It is your turn to hear me now. You are deluded, Romeo. Vampires do not have the capability to love. They are heartless and their only intentions are to kill."

"You are wrong," Romeo spat out as he sat up and wiped his bloodied nose with the sleeve of his shirt.

Mercutio helped Romeo up off the floor. "I am afraid he is right, and your father would wholeheartedly agree—not to mention skin you alive if he knew you were consorting with the enemy."

"So instead I should follow your example and consort with women who smell like a barnyard and taste like cheap whiskey?" Romeo said as he dusted himself off.

"Enough of this blathering. We have a good fifty or

more weapons to tend to," Mercutio said, and pointed to double bows that needed to be restrung.

"So do you plan on visiting a harlot's bed this evening, Mercutio? Is that why you are in a hurry?" Benvolio asked with a laugh.

Mercutio got out some wooden stakes and stacked them on the floor, readying them for inspection. "I wish. I had plans with Maribel, a servant maid from Capulet Castle, but she canceled because she has to work at that ridiculous ball for the prince. She'd promised me a foot massage, so I'm quite disappointed."

"She is better off serving food to those bloodsuckers than touching your calluses," Benvolio said.

"It depends on who this servant maid is," Romeo said, relieved that the tension in the air had lifted. "How ugly is she?"

Mercutio sneered at Romeo. "Maribel is not ugly, you imbecile. In fact, she's quite attractive. Even more so than her mistress, Rosaline."

Romeo's mouth hung open. "You are courting Rosaline's servant maid? Since when?!"

"Only a few days. But we haven't mentioned you and Rosaline at all, if that is what you are worried about," Mercutio said.

Romeo was thrilled by his friend's revelation. It was entirely possible this Maribel was a trusted confidante of Rosaline's. If he could somehow charm and impress the woman, perhaps she would speak kindly of him to Rosaline and convince her mistress to give him a chance. If he didn't act on this news now, he would regret it for the rest of his life.

"Tonight I will win Rosaline's favor," Romeo said with a renewed spirit. "And both of you are going to help me."

Mercutio narrowed his eyes at Romeo. "How do you propose we do that?"

"You will convince your pretty servant maid to sneak us into the ball so that I can see Rosaline," he answered.

"A few moments ago my lady friend was ugly, and now all of a sudden she is pretty," Mercutio said.

"Like I said, I'm full of surprises," Romeo said with a smile.

Benvolio did nothing to mask his frustration. "This is ridiculous, Romeo. And dangerous to the point of suicide!" he said. "We've never gone to the castle at night. The vampires will outnumber us by the hundreds."

But Romeo would not be persuaded by Benvolio's gift for reasoning. "We can go in disguise and blend into the crowd undetected. No one will even know we are there."

"This is the most preposterous plan ever created," Mercutio said, throwing his hands up in the air. "I refuse to take any part in it."

"So do I," Benvolio echoed.

"Well, if you don't come along, I will go to Capulet

Castle all by myself," Romeo said with confidence.

Benvolio and Mercutio traded an uncomfortable glance while Romeo waited for their response. Benvolio nodded, and Mercutio took a hefty wooden stake from the top of the pile, offering it to Romeo as though it were a family heirloom.

"We must shave a few of these down so they will fit underneath our coats," Mercutio said.

"And we will ask Friar Laurence for garlic and enough holy water to fill our ankle flasks," said Benvolio.

Romeo grinned as he shook their hands one at a time. "I suppose we must prepare for the worst."

"And for your innocence to be lost," Mercutio said with a wink.

CHAPTER THREE

From behind a tall limestone pillar near the top of a winding staircase, Juliet watched the festive scene unfold in the castle's Great Hall. Her eyes bounced around the candlelit room with great interest and curiosity, settling upon striking women in glittering, beaded ball gowns and stoic gentlemen dressed in long formal jackets, stitched with shimmering gold thread.

She was amazed by the civility of it all. Humans and Capulets, gallivanting together as if there hadn't been more than five years of bloodshed between them. It truly boggled the mind, but not enough to dampen the cheery mood of Transylvania's most elite humans, who obviously were curious about the country's most notorious vampires.

A choral trio was assembled in between two towering

marble columns, singing "Ave Regina" by Guillaume Dufay. The angelic sound of their high-pitched voices competed with the din of chatter in the air. Juliet had no need to wonder about the subject matter of people's conversations—the peace treaty that was threatening the tight choke hold the Capulets had over the region. Soon Prince Radu would arrive at the castle as the guest of honor and be welcomed by the most prestigious clan of vampires in all of Europe.

Juliet took a deep breath and felt her whalebone corset tightening against her rib cage. She knew she should be relieved by the prince's presence this evening. Originally, this ball was scheduled to take place three days from now in celebration of Juliet's sixteenth birthday, but plans had changed once Vladimir was imprisoned. The Capulets altered the theme of the dance and invited Prince Radu, hoping that they could prove they were worthy of the power his half brother had bestowed upon them, and persuade the prince to lift the treaty so their freedom to feed off of humans would no longer be compromised.

Juliet's extended family was so distracted by the political upheaval that they had seemed to forget all about her and her coming-of-age ritual. Juliet wished to put it out of her mind as well, at least for this evening. But when she felt a familiar warm, strong hand with long, sharp fingernails rest upon her shoulder, there was nowhere safe for her mind to go.

"Where have you been hiding, Juliet?" a deep, raspy voice asked.

She turned her head, and out from the shadows came the distinguished and handsome face of her father, Lord Capulet. She stood there frozen for a moment as she took in his mesmerizing features—a sharp square-set jaw, a well-kept beard, and dark red eyes that could burn holes right through her if she ever dared to disobey him. Juliet swallowed hard as she imagined her father as a young man on his sixteenth birthday, snapping the neck of an innocent human, then biting down into his flesh and sucking every ounce of blood from his veins.

"I'm not hiding," Juliet replied meekly. "I just needed to be alone with my thoughts for a moment."

Three young women, all around Juliet's age, passed by, giggling like they did not have a care in the world. Juliet watched as her father's red eyes tracked the girls. Lord Capulet's mouth broke into a wide grin, causing Juliet to shudder. She couldn't help but picture all the naive human women he must have lured into his lair with his charming smile and then "turned" into vampires with a swift, deep bite to their necks and a few drops of his blood.

The physical rush from turning humans into vampires was as strong as a dose of opium. The practice had run rampant in the vampire world for years, but it became less popular when their numbers grew and grew and there was not enough food to go around. Now with the peace treaty in effect, turning was also illegal, and those who continued to perform the act did so in absolute secrecy.

"You haven't been down to the ball yet," Lord Capulet said. "Why don't you tell me what's troubling you?"

"I'd rather not." Juliet knew confiding in her father was not a good idea. Sometimes his temper ran even hotter than Lady Capulet's.

"Your mother mentioned something. That you'd rather abstain from the initiation and die than become what you were meant to be." Lord Capulet stepped away from Juliet, his cape whipping behind him, and peered out over the top of the staircase as though he were a monarch looking down on his kingdom. "I didn't pay it any mind, given how hysterical women tend to be."

Juliet felt prickles of heat wash over her neck like a rash. Thankfully, it wasn't visible, because of the high collar of the emerald green gown her nurse had picked out for her this evening.

"Hysteria is the invention of men who aren't able to control their spouses and daughters. Frankly, I believe I'm the only one in this family with the slightest sense of what is right and wrong," she said tightly.

"Loyalty comes above all else, Juliet, even your

sense of morality, however misguided it may be." Lord Capulet kept his gaze trained on the merriment of the crowd downstairs; he was visibly unaffected by what Juliet had said to him.

A fit of anger bubbled up inside of her chest, which she was barely able to contain.

"Don't you mean *duty*, my lord?" Juliet's tone was even more pointed now. "With loyalty, a person has a choice of whether or not to stand by someone. For instance, by asking Radu here, you are choosing to betray your loyalty to Vladimir, are you not?"

Juliet was sure that her accusation would tweak her father's ego. The large bell in the north tower rang out five times, signaling that Prince Radu's horse and carriage had made it through the castle's main doors.

Lord Capulet bared his sharp fangs. Juliet moved backward, her hands trembling. She'd seen this menacing side of him many times before, and each instance was just as terrifying as the last.

Lord Capulet bolted toward Juliet, grabbing her by both arms, his nails leaving indentations near her elbows. "This willfulness of yours stops now. Do you understand me?"

Juliet's breath was coming in large gasps. By the possessed look in Lord Capulet's red eyes, she realized she'd upset him much more than she had intended. Juliet couldn't bring herself to speak, so she only nodded.

"You will help me and your mother show the prince that we are deserving of this castle and our riches and our right to survive! Or you will pay such a dear price that starvation and death will seem like a sweet reward to you."

Juliet could no longer look into Lord Capulet's rage-filled eyes. She bowed her head in submission and said, "Yes, Father."

A flood of applause carried throughout the rafters of the Great Hall. A booming voice called out, "Prince Radu of Wallachia and his sergeant at arms, Sir Felix." Lord Capulet let go of Juliet and inhaled deeply, putting one of his hands on his chest. His shoulders relaxed and the expression on his face went from agitated to serene.

Lord Capulet held out a hand and smiled once again. His fangs had receded, but still she was hesitant to go near him.

"Come, Juliet," he beckoned. "It is time to fight for our lives."

As Juliet wove her way through the crowd, reluctantly holding on to Lord Capulet's arm, acrid whispers were needling her ears. Her father seemed impervious to the noise, slowly floating above the marble floor with his chin jutting out and his fiery eyes locked on the raised platform where he was to meet Lady Capulet and greet Prince Radu. With her head hung low, Juliet tried to block the steady stream of voices from her mind, but they were impossible to ignore.

"Lord Capulet is fooling himself. He will never convince the prince to revoke his ruling," said a distant female relative who Juliet couldn't quite place. The woman shared Lady Capulet's high cheekbones, and from the look of her silken violet-colored dress, also the lady's impeccable taste in exquisite fabrics.

A statuesque, crimson-eyed man clutching a goblet filled to the brim with a dark red liquid seemed annoyed by her comment.

"For God's sake, look around you. He has turned our family into a dynasty, in spite of those scum-sucking Montagues. He is capable of anything, and charming anyone, including the prince of peace here."

The man put his nose up to the rim of the glass and inhaled, like one would do with a fine wine, but his lips pursed as though he smelled something repulsive.

He must have taken one of the large pewter cups full of pig's blood that the servants were passing around, Juliet thought. Since the treaty, all of the Capulets had been reduced to living off it. From the looks of things, this big change hadn't seemed to affect the vampires, but many believed that human blood was what made vampires so strong, and over time, the lack of it would substantially weaken them.

From the way her parents had been acting lately, Juliet figured the theory was true. Yet at the same time, she didn't want to believe it. While the peace treaty could not protect her from her initiation rite, Prince Radu had finally done what Juliet had never been able to do—stop her family from harming people. Not only that, it would certainly discourage the Montagues from hunting her vampire relatives down, now that they would be facing a death sentence.

Still, Juliet believed that the Capulets feared losing their political power, social rank, and affluence more than losing their physical prowess. Without their superhuman strength, they would not be able to guard any of it.

So it wasn't just the lack of bloodlust that separated her from the rest of the Capulets—it was also her lack of greed.

As Juliet walked toward the platform at the head of the Great Hall, she tried to settle her thoughts, but the twittering of the crowd had become more insistent.

"This treaty might just redeem their souls, don't you think?" a brunette-haired maiden chirped, her limestone crucifix pendant catching the light emanating from the candelabras on the ceiling. All the human guests at the ball were wearing one type of cross or another around their necks—doing so would make their bodies hot as fire to any vampire who dared touch them. It was certainly a bold reminder to the Capulets that they were far from being trusted.

"Do you honestly believe a diet of pig's blood and a

signed scroll is going to bring out the good in them? We're better off letting the Montagues hunt them to extinction, which will be easy once their bodies are weakened," her short and pudgy male escort replied.

Juliet swallowed hard. Perhaps the treaty would not be so effective in protecting her family as she'd thought. As she took a few more steps forward, her father's strong hand tightly clamped over her own, she shut her eyes briefly and tried to clear her mind.

When she opened them a moment later, Lady Capulet was within view, as well as Prince Radu and his highest-ranking knight, Felix. Juliet never believed she would find anyone more intimidating than her mother, who stood so straight and rigid that she appeared to be a good ten feet tall. However, the longer Juliet looked at the prince, with his salt-colored hair, pink windburned cheeks, and virtuous-looking pale blue eyes, the more in awe of him she became.

Once she and Lord Capulet ascended the platform, Juliet could also see that the prince was wearing a red military-type uniform, which was similar to that of his sergeant at arms, only slimmer in the shoulders and more decorated with medals. Everything about him demanded respect, especially the brutish, scowling Sir Felix, who made no effort to conceal the long-sword at his side.

When her father bowed before the prince, Juliet lowered herself into her most reverent curtsy, her gown rippling around her like a wave of green spring leaves.

"Good evening, Prince Radu. We are delighted to have you and Sir Felix at our home," Lord Capulet said.

"Thank you, good sir." Prince Radu raised his eyebrows in amazement as he watched Lord Capulet levitating above the floor, right next to Juliet. "I am pleased to be here among your family and . . . shall I say 'friends'?"

"Acquaintances mostly, but future allies, I hope." Lord Capulet extended his hand to a lavishly dressed Lady Capulet and guided her to his left side. "You already met my lovely wife at the gate."

"It is a great honor, Prince Radu," Lady Capulet said as she delivered a perfect floating curtsy. Juliet was surprised that her mother could even get back up—the onyx choker around her neck was so gigantic, it must have weighed twenty pounds.

"And this is our precious daughter, Juliet."

Juliet stifled a sarcastic laugh. If anyone had caught her with her father a few minutes ago, they would have questioned his use of the word "precious."

Nevertheless, Prince Radu smiled at Juliet and planted a gentle kiss on her hand.

"It is a privilege to meet you, Your Highness," Juliet said.

"The privilege is mine, young lady," the prince replied.

After a few moments of pleasantries, Juliet's father gestured toward the expansive Great Hall.

"Shall I show you around the castle before I present you to the rest of our company?" Lord Capulet offered.

The prince glanced around the room, taking in the artistry of the Gothic rose windows and beautiful hand-woven, wall-hanging tapestries all around him. "Yes, I'd enjoy that."

As Lord Capulet began to lead the prince and Sir Felix away, Juliet felt her mother's fingers lace through her own. A cold sensation traveled up Juliet's arm and deep into her chest. When in the presence of her mother, she usually was tense, but this feeling of dread was in a class of its own.

"Good God, I thought they would never stop talking. There is no time to waste," Lady Capulet said, pulling her daughter down the stairs of the platform with great fervor.

Juliet tried to writhe away from her mother's grip, but it was useless. Lady Capulet's strength matched that of her husband's.

"Where are you taking me?" Juliet asked.

Lady Capulet grinned, her teeth slightly stained with pig's blood. "You will see soon enough."

CHAPTER FOUR

omeo peeled back the hood of his gray cloak and gazed up at the foreboding mass of stone and brick that was Capulet Castle. Protected by a gigantic iron gate that seemed to reach into the clouds, the building stretched out for at least seven hundred yards and had four enormous towers from which a handful of guards with crossbows stood watch. Romeo was dumbstruck by its imperviousness. He could hardly believe that any Montague had ever breached these grounds, let alone launched a full-fledged attack on the vampires inside.

A fierce wind roared through the heavy brush outside the castle's perimeter, where Romeo, Benvolio, and Mercutio lay in wait, crouched down behind a swath of shrubbery under the light of a half-moon. Even though the fabric of his cloak was thick wool, a frigid chill ravaged his body and he shuddered. Then again, perhaps his nerves were just getting the best of him.

For over an hour, he had been waiting for a sign from Rosaline's servant maid, Maribel. She would turn on a gaslight in the last room to the left on the ground floor, once the secret door in the servants' quarters was unlocked. Romeo was deeply concerned that something was wrong. Although Mercutio was quite intelligent, he was known for getting involved with women who were pretty yet dim-witted—perhaps she had forgotten all about them. Romeo felt his hands beginning to shake. He had to distract himself.

"Did I tell either of you about the dream I had last night?" he asked in a soft voice.

Mercutio scratched at his neck with the handle of his parrying knife. "No, you did not."

"If it is about Rosaline and her half-breed bosoms, we are not interested," Benvolio said as he canvassed the area with a studious gaze.

"Speak for yourself." Mercutio nudged Benvolio.

Benvolio rolled his eyes and shoved Mercutio back with his elbow so hard that Mercutio fell into a pile of sticky moss.

"Take cover, Romeo. I'm about to punch Benvolio's lights out," Mercutio growled.

"Will you be quiet?" Romeo whispered. "You know how sensitive the vampires' hearing is."

Benvolio took a dagger that was hidden beneath his

sleeve and stabbed the ground near Romeo's feet, turning and twisting it until a mound of dirt and worms was wrought up from the topsoil.

"We could take them all on if we had to," he said.

Romeo shoved his hands into the pockets of his cloak. "Remind me to have a doctor take a look at you, Cousin. You're obviously delusional."

"Maybe he'll be committed to a sanitarium," Mercutio said snidely. "We'd all be better off."

"Actually, I could use some sanity right now," Romeo said. "That dream of mine was terrifying."

Benvolio's eyes widened. "Really? Go on."

Romeo glanced at Benvolio and Mercutio skeptically, knowing that they'd probably laugh at his story. But when he looked at the window again and saw nothing but pitch-blackness, he continued.

"I dreamed that my lady came and found me dead, impaled by Vladimir himself. Then I was brought back to life by her kisses on my lips."

"That does not sound so awful," Mercutio said.

"I agree, you survived in the end," Benvolio added.

"You do not understand. I was alive again, but . . . as one of them." Romeo nodded at the castle ominously.

"Don't worry, Romeo." Benvolio picked up a worm and let it crawl around in his open palm, then suddenly flicked it off with his finger. "If this dream came true and you were turned by one of those filthy monsters, I would put you out of your misery. I could not promise you that it would be painless, but rest assured, it would be quick."

Romeo crossed his arms over his chest and shook his head. "That is very thoughtful of you, Benvolio."

"Romeo, look! The light came on inside the castle!" Mercutio said, pointing at the room where the servant maid had promised to give them safe passage.

Romeo sighed in relief. "Thanks be to God."

"Do not thank God yet," warned Benvolio as he patted Romeo hard on the back. "This mission has only just begun. Who knows what will happen when we enter the vampire lair during dinnertime?"

"Stop being so dramatic," Mercutio said as he reached into a burlap sack and pulled out three garlic cloves attached to link chains. "Here, take these. Friar Laurence dipped the cloves in triple-blessed holy water and the chain is made of pure silver. This combination will render us invisible to both vampires *and* werewolves. But it only lasts for another hour, so Romeo, you and your wench cannot dawdle."

"One more foul word about Rosaline, and I will pummel you with my fist," Romeo snapped, ripping his string of garlic away from Mercutio and putting it around his neck.

"Actually, I think you should bludgeon him with this." Benvolio reached into the burlap sack and brought out a foot-long crowbar.

Romeo stared at it in sheer amazement. "What else do you have in that bag?"

"Just the usual—a handsaw, wooden stakes, a mason chisel, shears, and a couple of axes," Mercutio explained matter-of-factly.

"I suppose that will suffice," Romeo said.

"We cannot carry it all. That would only slow us down. Pick just one or two weapons and follow me." Benvolio snuck out of the bushes with cloves of garlic dangling around his neck and the crowbar in his right hand.

Romeo stuffed the mason chisel and a wooden stake into the waistband of his trousers and then darted off behind Mercutio, who was already ahead and walking stride for stride with Benvolio.

Romeo's heart started pounding as he and his cousin dashed across the outskirts of the estate, making their way toward the gate. Romeo kept his eyes trained on the tower guards to make sure they had not been spotted. Fortunately, no one seemed the slightest bit aware of the Montague trespassers. The necklaces must have been working.

"Here it is," Mercutio whispered. He halted in front of a warped section of the gate, where one of the bars was bent to the side, creating a small hole. "Maribel told me that when she steals away to see me, she slips through this spot here to evade the guards."

Benvolio examined the damaged gate and snickered. "Obviously she eats less than your last lady
friend. That boar could not have gotten through here
if she tried!"

Mercutio poked Benvolio in the stomach with the
handle of his mallet. "Neither will you, my paunchy
friend."

"Quit fooling around and step aside." Romeo
snatched the crowbar away from Benvolio, wrapping
his fingers around the base of it with all his strength.
"We have a party to attend."

Careful not to make any loud sounds that would
alert the guards, Romeo placed the crowbar between
the two metal rungs in the gate so he could get ample
leverage. He shifted his shoulders forward and then
leaned backward, hoping to pry the rungs apart even
farther so he and his cousins could sneak through.
However, his effort made little difference.

Romeo tried again, this time using both his arms
and his leg muscles with all his might. His palms
became wet with perspiration and his arms ached, but
he ignored the pain and thought of Rosaline—her gor-
geous, milk-colored skin and bright, beaming eyes. He
was so close to seeing her, he would not let anything or
anyone stand in between them.

Romeo dug deep into his soul for a surge of brute
power, and with one final swift, heaving motion, he bent
the metal rung so far that it almost snapped in two.

"Aha! I did it!" Romeo said, pumping a fist into the air in jubilation.

"Congratulations, Romeo. That only took forever." Benvolio rolled his eyes.

"Let's get on with this already," Mercutio said.

"I will lead the way," Romeo said as he handed the crowbar to Benvolio and stepped through the new partition in the gate. One at a time, Benvolio and Mercutio followed behind him, their feet swift and light on the ground.

"It is so dark out here. I can hardly see anything," Romeo said, using the ambient yellow glow from the servant maid's window to guide himself across the grounds.

Suddenly Mercutio stopped dead in his tracks. "Wait, did you hear that?"

"Hear what?" Romeo asked.

"It sounded like . . . growling."

Romeo remained still and listened. Other than the sound of rustling tree branches, he did not hear anything out of the ordinary. "It is just the wind, Mercutio. Carry on."

The trio picked up their pace, taking large strides toward the castle, but they did not get too far before Benvolio made an abrupt stop.

"Mercutio is right. Something is out here, watching us." Benvolio shifted his legs apart into a fighting stance and held the crowbar in an attack position.

Romeo could hear it now—a low, hungry growl that was seething with anger. He instinctively rubbed a garlic clove between his fingers. "Mercutio, you said we were invisible to vampires and werewolves."

A thin steam of moonlight illuminated two pairs of beady golden eyes and salivating mouths with sharp teeth.

"But not to dogs," Mercutio said, his voice wavering.

Romeo gulped as the two snouts sniffed the air for fear.

"This is bad," Benvolio said.

"Very bad," Romeo agreed.

Once one of the dogs had lunged at them, there was nothing left to do but—

"Run!" Benvolio proclaimed, and took off like a scared rabbit.

Without a second to lose, Romeo broke into a fast sprint, with Mercutio scrambling alongside of him and the dogs in hot pursuit. Romeo ran through a cluster of stone bunkers and over a wooden footbridge that crossed a small moat. Mercutio put forth a burst of momentum and dashed past Romeo, which annoyed him immensely.

With both his mates ahead of him, Romeo was tempted to look back and see how close the dogs were, but that would only slow him down. Besides, their ferocious barking was ringing in his ears, so he knew they were on his heels.

"This way!" Mercutio called out from a few feet ahead.

Romeo was running so hard he was barely able to breathe. He locked his gaze on Mercutio, who had reached the window of the ground floor and dropped to his knees in front of it. Mercutio quickly felt around a thick swath of grass with both hands, searching for the hidden door handle. He pulled the door open to reveal a secret entrance to an underground tunnel.

"Hurry!" Mercutio waved at Benvolio and Romeo.

Benvolio got there first, leaping into the entrance-way like a flying acrobat. Romeo was three or four steps away when he felt something tug hard at the bottom of his cloak. There was another sharp yank on his arm and he was dragged to the ground. While the dogs gnawed on his cloak, he tried to reach for the mason chisel he had lodged in the waistband of his trousers, but he could not grasp it. He said a short prayer, just in case he didn't survive the brutal mauling about to unfold.

Luckily for Romeo, the dogs let go of him willingly, in order to chase down large chunks of raw meat that had just been tossed into a row of rosebushes. He glanced up and grinned at Mercutio, who was standing above him with a light glaze of blood on his hands.

"Maribel's a smart one." Mercutio beamed. "She left some treats for the dogs at the foot of the door. I guess they haven't eaten in a while."

"Well, that much is obvious," Romeo replied. "Let's get out of here before they are ready for dessert."

Mercutio held a hand out to Romeo, and he took it in his, bloodied and all. When he was back on his feet, he gave Mercutio a heartfelt smile.

"Mercutio, I owe you my life," he said.

"Romeo, I am your friend. You owe me nothing." Mercutio placed a hand on Romeo's shoulder and grinned. "Now come on. You have a half-breed to woo."

Romeo smiled and shook his head, then followed Mercutio down into the secret tunnel.

CHAPTER FIVE

The life had practically been squeezed out of Juliet's hand when her mother finally let go. Lady Capulet had dragged her to the edge of the dance floor, where an older, impeccably dressed vampire floated at attention before her. As Juliet shook out her pink fingers, hoping to revive them, she became distracted by all the graceful couples who moved in choreographed unison to the music. But when she felt Lady Capulet nudge her forcefully in the shoulder, Juliet's eyes shot back to the man who her mother obviously wanted her to meet.

"I apologize for our tardiness, my lord," Lady Capulet said with a dutiful curtsy. "Welcoming the prince took longer than expected."

"Oh, an apology is unnecessary," the vampire replied as he stared intently at Juliet. "Although I'm setting eyes on her for the first time, I can already tell that meeting your daughter has been worth the wait."

Juliet stifled a laugh. The vampire's charm was so uninspired and clichéd, it was comical.

"Juliet, this is Count Paris. He has come a long way to see you," her mother said eagerly.

A flash of prickly heat was quickly visible upon Juliet's cheeks. This was certainly the same Count Paris who had written to her.

"Hello, sir," she muttered, and bowed her head in respect.

The count raised an expectant eyebrow and smirked. "Would you care to dance, Miss Juliet?"

"She would love to," Lady Capulet answered, gently pushing her daughter toward Count Paris.

Almost instantly, Juliet was swept away by the count for a saltarello, a courtly dance that included box steps, twirls, and promenades. Count Paris stood next to Juliet, then reached behind her and put his right hand on her waist. As Juliet extended her left arm out to the side, he took her left hand in his.

"I haven't danced in ages. This will be great fun," he said cheerfully.

Juliet gave him a faint smile. Somehow she felt that dancing with him would be quite the opposite.

And she was absolutely right. With each step, the count's grip on her waist became tighter and tighter. Sometimes, she swore that she could feel his nails clawing through the lace panels of her dress. But regardless of how uncomfortable she was, she managed to keep an airy expression on her face, because everyone at the ball—including a delighted Lady Capulet—was gawking at her as she danced in his arms.

"This music reminds me of my childhood in Bulgaria. My mother loves the sound of the panflute," Count Paris said in an attempt to make small talk. "Have you ever been there?"

"No, my lord. I'm afraid I haven't traveled much outside of Wallachia," she replied.

Count Paris ran his hand down her back. "I have a strong feeling that is all about to change."

Juliet glanced over at the performer who was currently blowing into the panflute, willing him to cease playing so that she could excuse herself from this awkward encounter. But from the way Count Paris was breathing heavily in her ear, she could tell that her partner wanted the music to last until the first hint of morning light.

"Your parents never mentioned how beautiful you are," the count murmured as he spun Juliet out to his left side and then back again.

She tried not to roll her eyes. "I suppose Lord and Lady Capulet do not like to boast."

Juliet did not have the heart to tell Count Paris that she knew little about him, other than what he'd revealed in the letter he'd written. Nor did she have the nerve to say that while the "blessing" of immortality—and perhaps even the quality of human blood—had kept vampires rather young and virile over the years, it didn't necessarily make all of them attractive. With his pointy chin, bulbous nose, and ears that stuck out like an elephant's, Count Paris was proof of that.

Still, Juliet was not as shallow and fickle as other maidens her age. She believed that a person's soul was to be loved above their physical appearance, which is why she found Count Paris's leeriness more disturbing than the large mole upon his chin. Apparently, the vampire in front of her was not the cordial gentleman he presented in his letter.

Count Paris led Juliet into a short promenade, floating slightly above the floor with a proud look in his blazing red eyes. "No one should be modest when describing you, my dear."

"You are most kind." Juliet tried to think of a reason to take leave of him—an ill-fitting shoe? a severe headache?—but whenever a dance step led her into her mother's line of sight, she resolved to continue on.

"What do you think of the ball so far?" the count asked, twirling her three times in a row.

Juliet steadied herself on her silver heels, which were a touch too high for her. "I suppose it's . . . nice."

"Only 'nice'?" Count Paris laughed. "I doubt that

your mother or father would be happy with that answer. They have worked so hard to impress the prince."

"Oh, I am very aware of that, my lord," Juliet said as she dipped under the count's right arm and circled around him.

"I'm not sure if you know this, but the prince and I have become very close as of late. I'm one of his most trusted ambassadors," the count said. "When Vladimir was thrown into prison, Radu wanted to hire someone to negotiate with the Capulets. There was no one better suited to take on this task than a vampire, of course."

"So do you think you'll be able to convince Radu to reconsider his ruling?" Juliet knew it was slightly rude to put him on the spot, but she hoped that his response would be no.

The count took her hands in his and gazed at an opulent gold ring with a sea green stone that sparkled on her right index finger.

"This is quite lovely. Is it aquamarine?" he asked, changing the subject entirely.

"No, actually, it's turquoise. My father gave it to me on my thirteenth birthday," Juliet said, sighing.

There was only one topic she was interested in hearing the man talk about, and he was obviously refusing to share his views with her. Did that mean he was uncertain of his abilities as a diplomat? Considering everything that was at stake for her family, Juliet was understandably curious.

"Well, you are worth spoiling," the count added as he kissed both her hands.

"What about the prince? Does he think Vladimir spoiled the Capulets? It will come as no surprise that my family is afraid of losing all of their wealth and power over the region."

Count Paris led her into another promenade. "I do not wish to talk about politics with you, Juliet."

"Why not? Because I'm a woman?"

"Just barely," the count snickered. "But that is not the reason."

"What is it, then?" Juliet said, anchoring her feet to the ground and not budging another step.

The count cast his iridescent red eyes upon her and smirked. "Because you truly aren't one of us . . . yet."

"Ah, I see. I won't be worth listening to until I can suck all the lifeblood out of some poor, unsuspecting person," Juliet said sharply.

The tone of her voice would have made most men flinch, but this vampire was still grinning from ear to ear. "That is not what I meant."

"Yes, it is," she huffed.

"Please, Juliet, I'd much rather talk about more pleasurable things," Count Paris said, pulling her in so close that their lips almost touched. "Like what you think about me."

Juliet wrestled away from his embrace, but the count held her by the elbows and stroked a small patch of her bare skin with his thumb.

"I'm afraid that I have no thoughts to share," she said plainly. "I know virtually nothing about you."

Thankfully, the flautist ended his song with a long, whistling note. Count Paris let go of her arms so he could join in the applause. Juliet sighed in sweet relief and hoped that she could make her exit soon.

"Well then, I suppose I must better acquaint you," Count Paris said, once the crowd began to bustle again. "Quite frankly, when it comes to me, there are only a few things that you need concern yourself with."

Juliet peered over her shoulder to see if her mother was trying to eavesdrop on them, and was elated to see that she was nowhere to be found. "And what are those?"

A servant passed by with a tray stacked with blood-filled goblets and Juliet winced when he reached for one. The smell of pig entrails made her incredibly nauseous. Count Paris took a long swig from the cup and blotted a stream of blood from his mouth with a white handkerchief.

"I come from one of the finest families in Europe. We live in a castle, much grander than this one, and Prince Radu has asked me to be chancellor of Transylvania. I hope my elevated status pleases you."

Juliet felt a knot forming in her stomach. The way

the count had just listed his assets could only mean one thing. "I'm not sure why any of that should matter to me, sir."

"Well, because in a few short days you will become my wife," he said with a broad smile.

"Wife?!" Juliet felt a rapid fluttering sensation inside her chest. This was exactly what she had feared when she read his stupid letter.

"I have it all arranged with your mother and father. An alliance between our families will help improve your father's relationship with the new prince, especially now, when so much is at stake. Once you complete your first kill and transition, I will take your hand in marriage. Then you and your family will have nothing more to worry about . . . ever."

Count Paris raised his eyebrows at Juliet, who just stood there, completely aghast. "Would you care to make a celebratory toast? I can hail another servant and get you some wine. But I should warn you, madam—after you have your first taste of blood, there's no going back."

A blistering sting spread throughout Juliet's entire body, one she'd never felt before. She wanted to get back at the count and her parents for using her as a bargaining chip in this twisted political game of theirs. Juliet imagined looking them all in their beady, red eyes and then spitting in their faces.

Fortunately, Juliet managed to squelch her rage

somewhat and rebuked the count in a more appropriate way. She grabbed his goblet, held it up, and proclaimed, "To wedded bliss!" Then she quickly poured all the contents over Count Paris's head, dousing him to the very last drop.

Her "fiancé" let out a startled yelp, alerting everyone around them to what had just happened. A group of socialites gasped at Juliet's outrageous behavior, while one of the dour-looking elder vampires shook his head and mumbled, "Lord Capulet will have her whipped when he sees this."

But he will have to catch me first, Juliet thought, and she sprinted out of the Great Hall to a place where no one would find her.

Underneath the ground floor of the castle ran four long, dark tunnels. The servants used them in the morning to access other rooms in the building without disturbing the vampires as they slept in their chambers; at night, the servants used them to evade the guards and exit the castle for an unscheduled evening of leisure in town. Originally, the tunnels had been constructed so that if the castle ever came under attack by the Montagues, the Capulets could move throughout the interior without detection and ambush their enemy. Some of the tunnels led to prison cells, where torture devices, like thumbscrews and knee splitters, were stored.

At the end of the south tunnel, there was a room such as this. It was about the size of two wardrobes, and Juliet would take refuge there whenever she clashed with Lord and Lady Capulet. She was on her way there now, weaving and darting through the underground system as she'd done countless times before. Since she had the routes memorized, she could navigate them easily in the near pitch-blackness.

The echo of her heels clicking against the slippery stone masked distant whispers that were being carried in the thin air. One woman's voice sounded familiar to her, but the others belonged to strangers. Juliet did not want to be caught in the bowels of the castle by the servants, so she picked up the pace, grabbing hold of the hem of her dress so it would not trip her up and swiftly ducking her head when she passed by places where the ceiling hung low.

After a good fifteen yards, she closed in on the secret room. Juliet opened the door and went inside. She reached into her shoe and pulled out a match, in hopes of lighting the oil lamp that she had brought down to the room a few days ago. She struck the match against the wall and it burst into a bright orange flame.

All of a sudden a terrified shriek rang out, startling Juliet so much that she toppled to the ground. A large black boot came out of the darkness, then a huge white hand with long, sharp fingernails. A set of wide red eyes became visible, along with a toothy grin that Juliet knew all too well.

"Tybalt? Is that you?" she whispered.

Juliet scrambled for the oil lamp that was in the corner of the room, lighting the wick just before the match extinguished itself. Her mouth went agape when she saw a busty blond woman, dressed only in her pink lacy undergarments, and her handsome cousin, putting his shirt back on.

"Don't you know how to knock?" Tybalt asked as he basked in the soft glow of the lamplight. "And stop staring at me like that. This isn't what you think."

Juliet put her hands on her hips. "Why do I find that hard to believe?"

Tybalt smiled at her as though nothing strange were going on. "Because you're too young, that's why."

"You said we wouldn't be found down here, Tibby," the lady whimpered.

Juliet let out a giggle. "Tibby, eh? Isn't that sweet."

"Be quiet, Cecilia!" he hollered into the cell.

Juliet gasped and kicked Tybalt hard in the shins, then stormed out into the tunnel, happy to hear her cousin groan in pain. Tybalt limped out of the room and stepped in front of Juliet, preventing her from leaving.

"What are you so upset about? She and I are just having ourselves a bit of interspecies fun. There's no law against that, is there?" Tybalt inquired while he buttoned up his shirt.

"You can be such a disgusting lout!" Juliet snapped, and stomped her foot.

Tybalt laughed and patted her on the head. "And you're still a little girl."

"I suppose that's why I'm down here, hiding," Juliet said, sighing.

"From your destiny, I presume?"

Juliet nodded.

"Well, I'm afraid you will never accomplish that. You are a Capulet, through and through, warts and all," he said, smoothing out his shoulder-length auburn locks.

"That may be, but there is one way to avoid my fate," she said, her voice serious.

"What, starve to death? Do not even threaten something like that." Tybalt's face suddenly filled with concern.

"Why not? If I get caught performing the ritual, I will be sentenced to death anyway, by the orders of Prince Radu," she replied.

"You won't get caught," Tybalt said. "I can tell you from experience that your natural, cunning instincts are strongest on your sixteenth birthday. You'll know in your bones everything you need to do." He peered over his shoulder at the practically naked young maiden in the cell. "You should trust me on this one."

Juliet rolled her eyes. "Like that woman in there trusts you? Please, I'm much smarter than that."

"Is that so?" Tybalt challenged her.

"You have her down here because you plan to turn her, but I bet she doesn't know that, does she?" Juliet said through clenched teeth.

Tybalt was not in the least bit offended by Juliet's accusation. He just grinned and said, "Guilty as charged, Cousin. But I have a feeling I'll be able to convince her that life as a vampire is much more interesting. Don't you agree?"

Juliet tried with all her might to push by Tybalt, but he would not allow her to escape.

"I'm sorry, Juliet. I don't know what else to do. Many of us are turning humans just to get by. It's the only way to get their blood without killing them," he said, his tone sweet as honey. "Come on, be nice. I hate it when you are cross with me."

Juliet remembered what she and Tybalt were like back when they were playmates. She had always been somewhat shy, but even so, she enjoyed Tybalt's rambunctious nature. But they were older now and Juliet had turned into a headstrong woman, while Tybalt became an overgrown child.

"Well, I do not feel like being nice, Tybalt! The peace treaty states that 'no harm should come to anyone.' What do you call this?"

"I don't believe that turning this woman into a powerful and immortal being is harming her," Tybalt said firmly. "Besides, the peace treaty is nothing but an act of tyranny leveled against our race. I should have the right to pursue liberty, satisfaction, and survival, like anyone else in Transylvania."

"Do I really need to point out that the Capulets are not like everyone else?"

Tybalt heaved a sigh of exasperation. "Why are you so argumentative? It is such an unappealing trait in a woman."

"It seems to work for my mother," she replied.

"Ah, well, that's probably who you get it from," Tybalt countered.

"Take that back. I am nothing like her!" Juliet said, shoving Tybalt in the chest.

"Yes, you are," Tybalt said, laughing. "You are both stubborn and hardheaded and determined to drive everyone around you insane."

Juliet shoved him again, so hard that he almost lost his balance. "That's a terrible thing to say. And it's not even true!"

"Oh, I hate to cut our conversation short, Juliet, but I should check on my lady friend. We must hurry along and return to the party before anyone suspects anything." Tybalt coughed into his hands in order to smell his breath.

"That's quite all right, Tybalt. I think we've talked long enough," Juliet said with all the sarcasm she could muster.

Since he'd transitioned, her cousin had been passionate about only two things—seducing women and killing Montagues, or whoever else Vladimir ordered him to obliterate. As she stared at Tybalt's cherubic-looking face, she wished that one day he'd wake up a kinder, gentler version of himself. Maybe then she'd be better able to put up with him and his teasing. But this was another one of those unattainable wishes that Juliet's nurse had warned her about.

"You won't see me or my companion down here again, Cousin, I promise," Tybalt said, grinning so that his pointed teeth were now visible.

An ominous sense of foreboding suddenly ripped through Juliet's soul and she could not shake it. Juliet knew in her heart that she never would see Tybalt down here again, but not because he was a man of his word. As Tybalt turned away from her and reentered the cell, Juliet dashed down the dark underground corridor, hoping to outrun all the fears that were closing in all around her.

CHAPTER SIX

With Mercutio and Benvolio right alongside him, Romeo took his first steps into the Great Hall, which was still filled to capacity with his family's longtime enemies. He strolled along the edge of the crowd, his posture confident and a topaz-colored cap hanging slightly over his eyes so that his face was partially obscured. His cousins were wearing similar hats, thanks to the generosity of Maribel the servant maid, who helped them with their disguises after the power of the necklaces wore off. Somehow, she had managed to acquire some very formal attire that was bulky and ornate enough to mask all of their identities—and their secret weapons. If Romeo had bumped into Benvolio or Mercutio in town wearing these silken capes and other accessories, he certainly wouldn't have recognized them.

While he surveyed the crowd for a glimpse of his sweet Rosaline, Romeo was relieved to see that the costumes they were wearing seemed to have fooled the Capulets. The vampires floated about, conversing with each other gaily, without noticing that the Montagues had infiltrated their soiree.

"So this is what these disgusting mongrels do when they aren't massacring innocent people," Benvolio mumbled as he monitored the vampires' every move.

"From the looks of all this commingling, it appears that peace in Transylvania might actually be achieved," Romeo said. He watched in amazement as two men on his left—one vampire, one human— chuckled with each other. Romeo never thought he'd see the day.

"Maybe you should keep your opinions to yourself until you've seen a Capulet murder someone you care about," Benvolio replied.

"It's not Romeo's fault that he isn't old enough to join us on the front lines," Mercutio said in his friend's defense.

Romeo gave Benvolio a cold, hard stare. "Honestly, I'm glad that I haven't fought in any of your battles. All it has done is turn you into a bloodthirsty savage."

"*I* am a savage?" Benvolio grabbed him by the arm, twisting his sleeve so tight that Romeo's wrist turned a bright shade of pink. "You better take that back."

"Or what?" Romeo taunted. He was sick of Benvolio's

bullying, especially now when he needed his cousin's help.

Mercutio suddenly broke in between them, holding two large chalices in his hands and smiling as though he'd just ingested a liter of ale. "Good fellows!" he said cheerily. "Stop bickering and be merry. We are among our dear friends!"

Then he shoved both glasses at Romeo and Benvolio, and quickly huddled together with them, whispering, "Who might try to tear us limb from limb if they find out who we really are."

Romeo realized Mercutio was right and reminded himself why he was putting all of them at great risk— the beautiful and perfect Rosaline. Arguing with Benvolio would only put his plan in jeopardy.

Romeo held up his chalice and grinned at Benvolio. "Agreed, Mercutio. We must behave as gentlemen."

Benvolio was still clearly angry, but he held up his glass anyway and tipped it politely toward Romeo. "That is the difference between you and me, Cousin. You consider yourself a gentleman, but I am now, and will always be, a warrior."

"I will drink to that." Romeo bowed to Benvolio, hoping to show his cousin some respect for his bravery, which could not be denied, no matter how Romeo felt about the violence between his family and the Capulets.

"And so will I," Benvolio said, his eyes gleaming a little.

They took a sizable gulp of their drinks. Instantly, they dropped their cups to the floor in horror, spitting the vile substance out of their mouths and onto Mercutio and his fine silken smock.

"My God, Mercutio! Where did you get this?" Benvolio said through a series of coughs.

Mercutio wiped some spit off his cheek with the back of his hand. "I took it from one of the servants' trays! Did the wine taste that bad?"

Romeo was coughing so much his eyes were watering. "Mercutio, this is not wine. This is . . . *blood*."

Mercutio's skin went as pale as the nearest vampire. "I suppose I should have taken a whiff of it first."

"I suppose I should wring your neck," Benvolio said, shaking Mercutio by his shirt collar.

Romeo was about to intervene when a tall and menacing figure glided toward them. Romeo had seen this vampire before, wenching and wreaking havoc at the pubs in town. His name was Tybalt, and as Romeo stared into his hellish red eyes, it seemed as though a moment of reckoning was upon them.

"Good evening, sirs. Is there something wrong with your beverages?" Tybalt asked in a simpering voice.

Romeo glanced at Benvolio, whose hand was dangling near his pocket, where he knew a small, blunt wooden stake was hidden from view. Romeo tried to remain calm and act in a jovial manner, but given how intimidating Tybalt was, it was difficult.

"No, not at all," Romeo replied in a cavalier tone. "They were just a little weak in taste."

Tybalt peered down at Romeo's goblet, his eyebrows rising with suspicion. "You certainly are adventurous. Most of our human guests prefer wine over pig's blood."

"Just like you, we are different from most humans," Mercutio quipped.

Tybalt gestured toward a servant, who came by with another tray of goblets and extended it toward Romeo. "Please try another. Perhaps yours was just tainted with parasites."

Reluctantly, Romeo reached for another goblet, his stomach rumbling at the thought of the foul taste the first sip had left on his tongue. Then out of the corner of his eye, Romeo saw a flash of chocolate brown. A young maiden with hair similar to Rosaline's had just melted into the throng of people standing around. Romeo's heart leaped into his throat, his passion winning out over sanity.

"Unfortunately, I must decline your offer," he said while trying to keep his eye on where the maiden wandered off to.

"And why would you do that?" Tybalt cracked his knuckles and smirked.

Romeo could see that Tybalt was looking for a reason to become aggressive, so he tried to placate him. He didn't have a moment to lose. Rosaline was most likely on the other side of the room—a new suitor was bound to approach her. "I beg your pardon, sir. I meant no offense."

"Do not beg for anything from him, Cousin," Benvolio said through gritted teeth. "This villain deserves nothing but a nice old-fashioned beheading."

Tybalt's smirk turned into a wide, sinister smile, his sharp teeth clearly visible as he growled like a wolf. He grabbed Romeo by the neck and brought him close so that Romeo's face was within devouring range. "You were crazy to think you could hide your Montague stench from me."

Mercutio sidled up to Tybalt, subtly pulling a dagger out of his jacket and pressing it against Tybalt's ribs. "Sorry to show up unannounced, but we were so distraught that we did not receive an invitation," he said.

Benvolio reached around to the back of his trousers and pulled out a sharp wooden stake, pointing it straight at Tybalt's chest. "Could you blame us? Our families have been so close over the years."

Tybalt's grip around Romeo's throat only got tighter. "Can any of you idiots count? There are three of you and three hundred of me. None of you are getting out of here alive."

Romeo was stunned by what was happening. In mere seconds, a roomful of Capulets could unite and rip him, Benvolio, and Mercutio to shreds. But when Prince Radu and his host, Lord Capulet, suddenly emerged from the crowd, Romeo realized he might be able to end this situation peacefully.

"Dear Prince! Lord Capulet!" he croaked as loudly as he could.

He caught their attention immediately, as well as the attention of Tybalt, Benvolio, and Mercutio, who were moments away from killing one another.

"Over here!" Romeo waved an arm above his head frantically, making a spectacle. The great Lord Capulet looked a bit skittish as he and Prince Radu approached.

"What is the meaning of all this commotion?" Lord Capulet said, seeming to be extremely displeased with Romeo's antics.

"My lord, these repulsive creatures are Montagues." Tybalt reluctantly let go of Romeo's neck and shoved him away. "I was just about to—"

"Introduce us!" Romeo interrupted, shaking Lord Capulet's hand before Tybalt could do or say anything else.

Lord Capulet and the rest of the lot gawked at each other, totally stunned.

"Is that so?" he asked, steeling a quick, uncertain glance at his nephew.

"Of course!" Romeo threw his arm around Tybalt as if they were childhood friends. "We were so happy that you extended an olive branch to us and requested that we join your celebration here. Weren't we, men?"

Benvolio and Mercutio looked at each other and

shrugged, putting their weapons down at their sides.

"And all of this is because of you, Prince Radu," Romeo went on, shaking the prince's hand. "You and your peace treaty have changed Wallachia for the better, and I for one applaud Lord Capulet for being such a strong proponent of it."

Prince Radu's eyes lit up, obviously pleased by what he'd just heard. "I applaud him, too." He turned to Lord Capulet and smiled. "This is a great achievement, and I am thoroughly impressed with your family."

Romeo looked at Lord Capulet, who at first had an indignant expression on his face, but soon it transformed into one of submission. "Thank you, Prince. We were hoping you would feel that way after being here and meeting us."

A vein in Tybalt's pale forehead pulsated as he punched the air in frustration. "This is preposterous! They are our mortal foes! They should be hanged or disemboweled for daring to set foot on our property."

"I thought I had put an end to those kinds of barbaric acts," the prince said to Lord Capulet, obviously dismayed by how Tybalt was behaving.

"Listen closely, Nephew. These men will remain at the ball and no harm will come to them," Lord Capulet said, staring Tybalt down. "Is that understood?"

A disgruntled Tybalt nodded in affirmation, then stalked out of the Great Hall without saying another word.

Lord Capulet turned in the opposite direction and held his arm out in front of him. "Come, Prince Radu. Let us join Count Paris in the courtyard. There is much for us to talk about."

Once Lord Capulet and the prince took leave of them, Benvolio and Mercutio doubled over in laughter, trying to catch their breath in between gasps.

"Romeo, I cannot believe you just did that!" Mercutio said as he clutched at his side.

"Leave it to you to talk your way out of being killed," Benvolio added. "I have never seen the mighty Tybalt sulk like a baby before."

Romeo, however, was too focused on searching for Rosaline to engage in his cousin's and friend's antics. Once again, his eyes drifted from woman to woman, seeking out the most delicate skin and most radiant smile he had ever encountered. After a brief moment or two, he noticed a petite maiden crossing the floor about fifty feet away. She was wearing a white-lace-and-emerald-green gown, which showed off an alluring figure that Romeo knew to be Rosaline's. He had fantasized about the curve that went from her waist to her hips almost every night before he went to sleep. Now was his chance to properly court her.

Romeo did not even think to excuse himself from his company. He just darted off into the crowd, slipping by vampire after vampire as though they were harmless. He did not even flinch as they floated through the room, their tongues licking dots of pig's blood from their lips and their eyes glowing bright red. All he could see was the back of Rosaline's head, her hair cascading down her shoulders as she halted in front of a marble column in the Great Hall and leaned up against it.

Romeo was only steps away from her when she turned around and looked in his direction. When her eyes locked upon him, he thought he might burn up with fever and die right there in that very spot.

At one time, the thought of dying might have troubled Romeo, much like his disturbing vampire dream from the night before. But all of a sudden he was no longer afraid of death. He was no longer afraid of anything. This delirious trance had rid him of every worry and filled him with a joy so all-encompassing that if he were to take his last breath before the sun came up tomorrow, his last words would be "Do not mourn me, for I have truly loved."

Romeo could not break away from the maiden's potent stare, and even if he could, he would not. Her face was that of a heavenly cherub, a perfect creation by the hands of God. Her eyes were like gemstones, glittering at the bottom of a deep blue sea. By the way she carried herself, he could tell that she was as graceful as a swan; and from the way she kept looking at him, he knew that her soul was meant to find his.

Without a doubt, this girl was Romeo's destiny, but she was not Rosaline Capulet.

CHAPTER SEVEN

"Good evening, my lady."

Four words. That is all it took to shake the protective wall around Juliet's heart down to its very foundation. A simple greeting, yet, at the same time, the most glorious thing she had ever heard a man say. It was the "my" that stuck with her. He had said the word as though he had been searching for her for many years, perhaps even his entire lifetime. This courteous and undeniably handsome gentleman—with soulful eyes, thin, pink lips, and a hint of stubble along his cheeks and chin—could not stop gazing at her either. Juliet had no idea that being singled out in a roomful of people could feel this wonderful.

But she knew better than to wear her heart on her sleeve. Over the last two years, her nurse had given her plenty of advice on how to relate to men, and the

number one rule was that women should be myste-
rious, coy, and say very little. Considering how dry
Juliet's mouth had suddenly become, not speaking
would be effortless indeed. She also remembered that
her nurse had mentioned that men loved the thrill of
the chase. But with her legs feeling as though they were
about to melt like the hot wax of a candle, she realized
that it was too late for her to run.

But why would she want to? One look at this man
and instantly Juliet hoped to stay with him—until
the moon and stars died, and all that survived was
sunlight.

"Are you waiting for someone?"

The sound of his voice was so full and melodic,
Juliet was mesmerized and still could not speak. She
just nodded her head in response.

"I see." He briefly lowered his eyes to his feet, then
engaged her with a small grin. "Well, I must admit, I
feel as though it is my duty to watch over you until your
suitor returns."

Juliet smiled back. "That is kind of you, sir, but
what makes you think I am waiting on a man?"

"Well, I, uh . . ." He trailed off and glanced up
at the sky as though he were praying for the right
answers. After a short pause, he looked Juliet in the
eyes, his smoldering gaze sending chills throughout
her body.

"I was going to say something about your stunning

beauty, my lady. But you appear far too intelligent to fall for flattery."

Juliet put her hand over her heart in hopes that she could slow it down. "That's probably the nicest compliment I have ever received."

"So have you ever been to a place with more nefarious creatures?" he said, peering around the room.

Juliet nearly laughed at the unintended irony of his question. "I suppose you are referring to the vampires."

"Not necessarily," he replied. Then he leaned in close and whispered into Juliet's ear. "I have a funny feeling that a lot of the humans here are lawmakers and politicians."

Juliet laughed. "You are probably right, sir. What, may I ask, is your profession?"

"Would you like to take a guess?"

Juliet tried to prevent herself from revealing her attraction to him, but she couldn't help herself. She was smiling too much, staring too long.

But then again, so was he.

"Well, you are not a vampire, so that is one point in your favor," she said.

"And thankfully neither are you," he said cheerily.

Juliet started wringing her hands and biting her lower lip, two detestable habits that both her nurse and mother chided her for. Obviously he hadn't noticed her paling skin, or that she wasn't wearing a cross pendant like all the other humans here. What would he think when he found out the truth? He would certainly forsake her—any human would do the same.

"However, I am not a prince, so I suppose that is one point against me," he joked.

"Two points, actually. You also smell like garlic," Juliet quipped, but instantly regretted her words. He must think she was the rudest woman on the face of the earth!

However, the gentleman who stood before her did not seem to care. "That's what I get for keeping cloves of it in my pocket."

Juliet could not recall when she last felt this alive. Was it months ago? Or never?

"To be honest, I'm working for my father. Temporarily, that is," he continued.

"Why is that? Do you not like the work?" she inquired.

The gentleman looked down at his feet and nervously rubbed the back of his neck. "No, I don't."

Juliet sensed that she had brought up a delicate subject, but for some odd reason, she felt very comfortable asking him to say more. "Is it because the two of you don't get along?"

"Not really. My parents have been out of the country since the peace treaty was passed," he explained. "They are taking a much-needed vacation in Serbia."

Juliet let out a light laugh. "I couldn't be more jealous."

"Because of their vacation?" he asked brightly.

"No, because you are free of your parents for a while."

The gentleman's lips curled up into a dashing smile. "I have to admit, it is quite liberating being without them."

"Or their rules," Juliet added, her eyes beaming.

He nodded in agreement. "Or their criticisms and unrealistic expectations."

"Or the plans they make for you without your consent, or the way they patronize you when you talk, or . . ." Juliet trailed off, realizing a little too late how bitter she must have sounded.

So much for her nurse's lessons in flirtation.

Thankfully, the gentleman was not turned off by her complaining at all. He just gave her a reassuring grin and said, "It seems to me that your parents do not know how lucky they are."

Her cheeks flushed several shades of pink. "Perhaps."

Suddenly their eyes locked and they were silent for a moment. Juliet could feel her body temperature rising as she gazed at him—she had the strangest feeling that she'd known him all her life.

"What about you? Are you going to inherit the family business someday?" the gentleman asked, breaking

Juliet out of her thoughts.

"If my parents have their way, yes," she said.

"Ah, I could tell from across the room that you were a rebel."

Another one of the gentleman's wide grins nearly melted Juliet's heart.

"Is that so?" she replied. "What else could you tell?"

"That you are a passionate person," he said with an intense stare that practically had her spellbound. "That you stand up for what you believe in."

"What else?" she murmured.

The gentleman inhaled deeply, like he was about to dive underwater. "That you need someone to be on your side. Always. Regardless of the circumstances."

Juliet was in such awe of this magnificent creature, and his ability to see right through her, that she was rendered speechless.

"I suppose I shouldn't say such things when your suitor could be lurking around the corner," he said.

Juliet's pulse was racing uncontrollably. "Actually, I do not have a suitor."

"I am surprised, but so very relieved," he was quick to say, his eyes brightening the room like flashes of lightning in a midnight sky. "Though I would have fought him for you if he had existed."

Juliet quickly shifted her gaze away from him. While other women might have found his words romantic, she didn't particularly like the idea of anyone fighting over her. There was too much turmoil in her family already.

The gentleman took Juliet's hand in his, noticing how quiet she had suddenly become. "I only meant to say that I would try to win your heart."

Juliet's skin tingled on the softest part of her palm. She sighed as she glanced down at their hands and how their fingers were intertwined, but when her eyes drifted toward his jacket, she saw a wooden stake sticking out of an inside pocket.

"What is that, my lord?" Juliet gently slid her hand out of his grasp and gestured toward the object.

His eyes immediately became cloudy. "Oh, this? It is just . . . a family heirloom."

"Wouldn't an embroidered handkerchief be more appropriate for the occasion?" Juliet mocked him playfully.

"Perhaps, but everyone in my family carries one of these. I know it seems strange, but when you meet my family, you will understand."

He reached for her hand once again, and Juliet could not pull away, even though she could hear her nurse's voice ringing inside her head, practically begging her to. The magnetism between them was immeasurable.

"And they will adore you as I do," he said, pressing his lips to her fingertips.

"Pardon me, my lady," a voice chirped from behind Juliet.

She used all the strength in her body to take her eyes off of this extraordinary man, craned her head over her shoulder, and met the glowering stare of her nurse.

"Can you not see that I am in the middle of a conversation?" Juliet asked.

"Yes, and I do hate to intrude." The nurse took Juliet by the arm and yanked her hand away from Romeo. "But your mother is requesting your presence at once."

"I am sure whatever it is can wait a few minutes," Juliet said pleasantly, wishing she had her mother's ability to make things disappear.

"I'm afraid not." The nurse stepped in between Juliet and the man, and said to him, "We bid you adieu, sir."

"Adieu, ladies," he said with a cordial bow.

Within moments, the nurse had pushed and pulled Juliet through the crowd and out of the Great Hall. Juliet was so furious, it almost made her dizzy. Once they reached the castle's orchard, which was currently deserted except for the fruit flies, she broke free of the nurse's clutches and let her have it.

"How dare you humiliate me like that!" she cried, her cheeks flushed with shame.

"Believe me, if I had not interrupted, you would have suffered far worse," the nurse shot back.

"What do you mean? That gentleman was nothing short of perfect!"

"Juliet, that gentleman was Romeo Montague," the nurse said firmly.

"You . . . you must be mistaken." Juliet could barely hear her own voice. It sounded faint and weak, like a phantom echo from another time and dimension.

"It is the truth, child. I swear it."

Juliet didn't need to look the nurse in the eyes to know she was being honest. She covered her face with her trembling hands and surrendered to the waves of grief that were suddenly crashing down upon her.

There was no way in hell that a Montague would have anything to do with a half-breed, let alone a full-fledged Capulet vampire. Not only that, but when Juliet thought of Romeo and his "family heirloom," she couldn't stop herself from imagining how many of her kin had been executed with something just like it. The weight of this revelation was just unbearable.

"Please, Nurse, do not follow me," Juliet murmured. Then she whipped around and ran out of the orchard with tears rolling down her face.

CHAPTER EIGHT

Romeo was dumbstruck when the girl and her nurse disappeared around the corner while his body was still bent at the waist in a bowing position. He was clueless as to why the nurse had disrupted their unexpected rendezvous, but one thing was certain: he had to uncover the girl's identity so that he could see her again. Romeo glanced at the people who were scattered around him, searching for Benvolio and Mercutio, but all he saw were ruby-colored eyes and skin as white as snow.

A determined Romeo decided to approach the most reserved-looking vampire: a petite golden-haired woman dressed in a black gown. She was sitting quietly on a purple settee, observing the crowd. The corners of her mouth turned up when Romeo came before her and bowed. This respectful gesture was probably a bit much, but he was willing to swallow some of his pride in order to learn the name of the woman who he wanted by his side for the rest of his life.

"I am sorry to trouble you, my lady, but did you happen to see me and a young maiden talking over there?" he asked.

"Yes, I did," she replied.

Romeo swallowed hard. "Do you perchance know her name?"

The woman's eyebrows raised, but not one wrinkle formed on her forehead—another perk of immortality, Romeo thought.

"I was wondering why you were pursuing her to begin with. But now this makes perfect sense. You are unaware of who she is."

Romeo became defensive at the caustic tone of the vampire's voice. "On the contrary, I know everything I need to, with the exception of her name. Please, do not toy with me."

"Or what?" The woman snapped, leaning forward in her chair and glaring at Romeo. "You will pull out a wooden stake and run it through my heart, just like your father did to my father?"

Apparently, Romeo's disguise was not as good as he had thought. A part of him wanted to apologize to this woman on behalf of the Montagues. But when he recalled how the Capulets had butchered and fed off of thousands of innocent people, his urge to make amends quickly vanished.

"No. I will simply take leave of you," he said, backing away.

The woman's haughty smile returned to her face as she declared, "Her name is Juliet . . . and she is Lord Capulet's only daughter."

Romeo stumbled over his own two feet, but he was able to catch himself before spilling onto the ground. The woman of his dreams was not just a Capulet—she was the child of his father's worst enemy.

"Juliet," he said to the vampire, his voice faltering a bit.

"In three days, she will fully become one of us." The vampire's tone was quite jovial now that she could see she had succeeded in rattling Romeo. "Does she know who you are?"

Romeo felt as though his throat was going to close up. He could not bring himself to respond.

"I can guarantee that when she finds out, you will be dead to her," the woman crowed. "Like all her kin who have died at your family's hands."

Staring into this vampire's vindictive eyes, Romeo almost considered showing her the wooden stake hidden under his jacket, but he was above making threats. Instead, he walked away, out of the Great Hall and through the long hallways and lanes until he reached a courtyard with an orchard. He hoped he could be alone there and compose himself.

Romeo was about to collapse onto a stone bench when he heard the sound of two very familiar voices coming from behind a wall in the orchard.

"Romeo! My cousin Romeo!"

It was Benvolio, bellowing like a senseless lout. Romeo shook his head in frustration, hoping that he would not be discovered. The last thing he needed was more ridicule from his friends.

"Be quiet, man. He is probably in bed with the half-breed, having his ears nibbled on." Mercutio chuckled.

"Wouldn't she be more interested in his arteries?" Benvolio asked.

"You're right," Mercutio replied.

"Maybe we should search upstairs, where the bed-rooms are," said Benvolio.

"Actually I think I have had enough of the house of the damned for one night. Romeo can find his way home on his own," Mercutio responded.

"Yes, we might have helped Romeo sneak into the castle to romance one of these bloodsuckers, but I want nothing more to do with them," Benvolio said in agreement.

Romeo listened closely as the sound of Mercutio's and Benvolio's footsteps tapered off into the starry night. He leaned back against the wall and ran his hand through his hair, wondering what his cousin and good friend might do to him if he revealed that he had fallen for the daughter of the most powerful bloodsucker of them all. But he was snapped out of his thoughts by the sound of window shutters opening three stories above him. His eyes darted upward and his mouth broke into a smile. Standing on a balcony, her face partially illuminated by the light of the moon, was Romeo's new reason for living.

"Juliet," he gasped.

Moments ago, Romeo was shocked to learn of Juliet's bloodline, but none of that seemed to matter now. In fact, he was so happy to see Juliet's face that he nearly ran out from behind the latticed fence and proclaimed his love for her.

But then common sense reeled him back. Here he was, enamored and heartsick and consumed by desire, but did Juliet return any of those feelings? Or would she hate him when she learned that he was a Montague? Or worse, be too far gone in her transition from woman to vampire to see him as anything but a source of human blood? Until he knew with absolute certainty, he would not make another move or utter another word or think another thought.

But he would allow his eyes to watch and his ears to listen, until his heart was fully satisfied.

Or until he became undone.

CHAPTER NINE

s Juliet stepped out onto her balcony, the ruffled skirt of her dress rippled in the evening wind. On mild nights like these, she liked to duck out of her chambers and onto this tiny terrace that stood above the orchard. It was so easy for her to find peace and contentment out here. Inside the castle, Juliet oftentimes felt trapped, but when she could escape to this little ledge outside her bedroom, her spirit soared.

Now the scent of pear trees wafted through the air, and the stars above her glittered like moon dust, yet Juliet was anything but content. Her cheeks and neck were blotchy from stress. When her head wasn't throbbing, her heart was beating so hard she felt like she couldn't catch her breath.

All because of a man she could not stop thinking about—and a man who was also a Montague.

"Oh, be some other name," Juliet said as she watched a comet's tail streak the sky with a brilliant white light. "But if this Montague swears his love to me, I will no longer be a Capulet."

There was a sudden noise in the orchard—perhaps a lark flying from one tree branch to another—but Juliet ignored it, too lost in her thoughts.

"Oh, Romeo, if you went by another name, I would adore you no less. But can either of us dismiss the facts?"

Another sound came from the ground below. This time, it was louder and caught Juliet's attention. She briefly peered down into the darkness, wiping a stray tear from her eye. But she saw nothing out of the ordinary.

"It is impossible to ignore or forget the history between our families. The stories I have heard about how my uncles have brutally slain your cousins. The vicious Montague raids that Tybalt protected me from again and again.

"My heart is not prejudiced, my dear, but my mind—"

"Is as alluring as your face," said a booming voice from within the orchard's walls. "And as sharp as your wit."

Juliet stumbled back a bit, completely stunned by the abrupt interruption.

"Who's there?" she asked.

"Apologies, my lady, but I heard you speaking on your balcony and could not spend another moment in silence," the voice replied.

Juliet covered her mouth with both her hands. This was so embarrassing.

Unless perhaps . . .

"Identify yourself, please, sir." Juliet approached the terrace banister and leaned over so she could have a closer look.

A gentleman stepped out from behind a lattice fence in the far corner of the orchard. He came into view when he took off his hat and gazed up, the moonlight striking the familiar and flawless contours of his face.

Juliet would have been thrilled to see it was Romeo, had she not just made a total fool of herself by revealing all of her feelings. What a disaster.

"I can only imagine what you must think of me," she said, her voice quite timid. "Now you know I'm a Capulet, and you have seen me talking to myself like an idiot."

Romeo placed his hat back on. "I have no ill will toward you, Juliet. And I don't care what either of our families has done to each other. I only want to make you happy."

"How did you find me here?" Juliet said with a smile so big, her cheeks hurt a little.

"It was by chance," Romeo said, his eyes never

drifting away from her. "But from now on, I will no longer leave our fate up to the whims of the universe."

Juliet's smile suddenly began to fade. "I'm afraid our fate is doomed, my lord, regardless of how we feel."

"Why is that? Because I am a Montague and you are a Capulet?"

"Yes, of course." Juliet bowed her head sadly. "How can we ever get past that?"

"Sweet Juliet, I personally have never taken the life of any Capulet," Romeo said eagerly. "Nor anyone else, for that matter. And I am certain you can say that you have never struck another person, whether they were Montague or not."

Juliet nodded in affirmation, although she knew that in three days, she would be expected to do far worse than that.

"Then why must we judge ourselves by the sins of our fathers? Why must we hate because they hate? Our love, Juliet, should be as free as we allow it to be," Romeo reasoned.

"*Our* love," Juliet repeated, her heart dancing.

"Oh, Juliet, please don't be doubtful," Romeo pleaded.

"It is not that simple." Juliet wished that she could let her emotions run wild, but one of them had to act reasonably.

"What else could come between us?"

"What else? I am turning into a vampire! In three days, no less." Juliet looked directly at Romeo to see his reaction, and much to her surprise, he was unfazed.

"If you were turning into a fish or a monkey or a chicken in an hour, I would not care," Romeo said, smirking.

"That is absurd." Juliet laughed in spite of herself. "And I do not know how you can find this funny!"

"I do not understand it either. But absurd or not, when it comes to these feelings I have for you, the last thing I want to do is ask questions," Romeo said.

Then he got down on one knee, and added: "Except for one . . . Will you marry me?"

Juliet felt like her whole body was weightless, and that any moment now, she'd float up into the clouds.

"I pledge all that I have and am to you." Romeo continued to talk as Juliet remained in a daze.

Out of the blue, a high-pitched voice arose from within her chambers. "Juliet! Miss Juliet!"

"One moment, good Nurse," she yelled over her shoulder. Then she quickly looked down at Romeo, who was still on one knee beneath her terrace.

"My love, if you must leave before you can answer, give me some small sign of hope," Romeo begged.

"Madam! I will not call you again," the nurse proclaimed in agitation.

The tension in the air had Juliet's stomach in knots.

She could barely think straight, so the only thing to do was listen to her heart.

"My darling, I must go. And so should you, before one of the guards catches you here. Then our marriage will never see the light of day," she said.

Romeo grinned and sprang to his feet. "So then you will marry me. Oh, blessed, blessed night!"

"MADAM JULIET!" the nurse shouted once again.

"I hear you! In a moment, I will come!" Juliet yelled back.

"First thing in the morning, I will ask Friar Laurence at the monastery to officiate at the wedding ceremony," Romeo said quickly.

Juliet had never fought so hard to contain her emotions. "And I will send someone to confirm the plan. I pray that sleep will not change your mind, nor mine."

"Do not make me curse at you, madam!" the nurse bellowed from Juliet's bedchamber.

Then Juliet blew Romeo a kiss and waved good-bye before making her retreat.

"How could you have done such a thing?" Lady Capulet scolded as Juliet sat on the edge of her bed with her hands folded meekly in her lap.

If she had known that the nurse had been beckoning her so that she could get verbally assaulted by both of her parents, Juliet would have jumped off the balcony and eloped with Romeo right then. But no, she would have to endure their ranting until they were satisfied with Juliet's apology for pouring the goblet of pig's blood over Count Paris's head. Considering that she was not even a slight bit remorseful, Lord and Lady Capulet could be there all night. The nurse, fortunately for her, had made a clean getaway.

"I admit, I might have overreacted a little," Juliet said. "But I had just found out that he and my parents were conspiring behind my back!"

"Do you realize what kind of position this puts us in?" Lord Capulet snapped, his fiery eyes brimming with anger. "Count Paris is an essential part of our strategy against Prince Radu's treaty. Now we are at an extreme disadvantage because of you!"

Fueled by newfound love and a burgeoning anger of her own, Juliet stared down her father and challenged him.

"Had you told me that you were arranging my marriage, then perhaps none of us would be in this situation," she fought back. "I am perfectly capable of choosing a mate!"

"That has nothing to do with it," he replied. "I am going to retrieve Count Paris from the Great Hall and bring him here so that you can ask for his forgiveness."

As soon as Lord Capulet stormed out of the room, Juliet sprang up and hollered after him, her poise cracking under the pressure.

"I am so tired of your orders!"

Lady Capulet gripped Juliet by the wrist and spun her around. "And we are tired of your disobedience! Your marriage to Count Paris—"

"Will be a complete fraud," Juliet interjected. "I do not even know him, let alone love him."

"Love?" Lady Capulet almost laughed. "What do you know about it?"

After meeting Romeo tonight, Juliet could have written volumes on the subject of love, but she would never admit that to her mother.

"I could ask you the same question," Juliet mumbled.

But Lady Capulet and her exceptional hearing caught every word.

"I know it must seem like I do not love you. Neither I nor your father is able to express those feelings easily," she replied. "But we care about you, and want what is best for you and this family."

Juliet lowered her head. The anxiety was finally getting to her. "Then why are you and Father hurting me so much?"

"These are difficult and trying times for our people." Lady Capulet let go of Juliet's wrist and lightly rubbed her daughter's shoulder. "We have to make certain sacrifices in order to preserve our lifestyle."

Juliet looked back up at her mother, her eyes glistening with tears. The thought of sacrificing her love for Romeo and all of her principles instantly weakened her.

"Is there no other way to curry favor with Count Paris? Or am I just that expendable, Mother?"

Lady Capulet sighed with resignation, but did not speak. Perhaps her daughter's pleas were beginning to sink in.

Juliet sensed an opportunity to sway her mother, so she took Lady Capulet's hand and kissed it as though her mother were a queen.

"Please, my lady, be lenient with me. Nothing in my life is in my own hands, and that is completely unbearable."

After a brief silent pause, Lady Capulet said, "Maybe we haven't examined all of our options with the count."

Juliet broke into a hopeful smile. "Does that mean you'll reconsider?"

Lady Capulet whisked herself away from Juliet and floated toward the door. "It means that I will speak to your father about it."

"Thank you," Juliet said with a dignified curtsy. She knew better than to push her mother any further.

"I'll send in your nurse to help you freshen up," Lady Capulet said as she exited the room. Once she reached the hallway, she glanced over her shoulder and added, "You still have a heartfelt apology to deliver, don't you?"

"Yes, Mother," Juliet said, crossing her fingers behind her back.

CHAPTER TEN

**R**omeo had never been happier to see Friar Laurence than he was the following morning. When he'd knocked on the door of the monastery, he was near delirious, having not slept a wink all night. Friar Laurence did not seem as excited to see him, however. It was just after six and everyone in the monastery was most likely still asleep. Nonetheless, Romeo knew the kind friar would welcome him into his home with a smile upon his face, regardless of the ungodly hour.

"Good tidings, Friar! Is this not the most glorious day in the history of time?" Romeo exclaimed, grabbing the man by his twiglike arms and shaking him happily.

Friar Laurence, a thin, older gentleman who barely filled his order's signature brown hooded robe, stifled a hearty yawn. "Why, how am I supposed to know, given that the day has only just begun."

"Not for those of us who have watched the sun rise," Romeo said, grinning. "Can I come in?"

"Of course you may." Friar Laurence opened the door and let Romeo enter.

"Thank you, Friar."

Friar Laurence left the door open a crack and led Romeo down the hall to a small, simple kitchen, where a black metal pot sat on top of a cast-iron stove. A steady stream of steam rose above it, leaving the room smelling like cinnamon and oats.

"Well, you are still in one piece, so I take it the holy-water-soaked garlic strands worked at the Capulets' ball," he said.

"They were very useful against the guards," Romeo replied. "I wish the same could be said of the watch-dogs, though."

Friar Laurence cringed. "How could I have forgotten them?"

"Senility perhaps?" Romeo joked. "Don't worry, Friar. We escaped the beasts with nary a scratch."

"What a relief," said Friar Laurence.

"We also adhered to the letter of Prince Radu's law," Romeo said proudly. "No violence ensued."

"Praise be to God, that is wonderful news."

The friar wandered over to the pot and stirred the contents with a wooden spoon. Romeo followed him, but stopped cold when he caught his reflection in a brass kettle. He had spent the late hours of the night stargazing in his favorite pasture, so he should not have been surprised to see dark circles under his eyes and slivers of grass tangled in his hair. What amazed him was how invigorated and intoxicated he felt, despite his haggard appearance. Truly, the joy that Juliet had brought into his life had infected every cell of his body.

"Are you hungry? I made some porridge." Friar Laurence poured some of the hot mixture into a bowl.

"No, my belly is just as full as my heart!" Romeo said. "I could go months without food, but not a single day without my lady."

"Ah, spoken like a man who has been struck by a thousand of Cupid's arrows." Friar Laurence smiled and then took a bite of the porridge. "I am glad that Rosaline finally came around."

For a moment, Romeo became worried about what Friar Laurence might think about his proposal to Juliet. But then he recalled how understanding the friar had been when Romeo had told him about his feelings for Rosaline weeks ago. She was a Capulet, just like Juliet, so his concerns quickly drifted away.

"Rosaline was nothing but passing fancy, Friar," Romeo said. "I never even saw her at the castle."

"Forgive me, Romeo, but I am baffled," the friar said with a full mouth. "If Rosaline hasn't caused this love-spun madness in you, then who has?"

"Her cousin Juliet."

Friar Laurence almost choked on his porridge, slapping at his chest in order to get the last bit down his throat. "You mean Lord Capulet's daughter?"

Romeo did not like the disapproving tone in Friar Laurence's voice. "Does it matter to who she was born? You have always said that we are all children of God, including the vampires."

"Son, I am not judging you," the friar said, laying a reassuring hand on Romeo's cheek. "Nor do I want to discourage your feelings for this girl. I am just surprised is all."

Romeo put an arm around the friar and grinned. "I am so happy to hear you say that, because Juliet and I are to be married. And I would like you to perform the ceremony—today."

The friar set the bowl down on the table and kept quiet.

"Well? What do you think?" Romeo prompted.

"I'm sorry, I'm at a loss for words," the friar replied.

"There is only one word to say," Romeo countered. "Yes!"

But Friar Laurence just stood there, motionless.

"Juliet said it rather easily, Friar. I do not know what is stopping you," Romeo said lightheartedly. He hoped a joke might cut the tension that was suddenly filling the air.

"I will not lie to you, Romeo. I don't know that this is a good idea."

"And why is that?"

"Your crush on Rosaline was naive and innocent, which made it all the more safe," the friar explained. "I know you are enamored with Juliet, but marriage is a serious undertaking, and you are quite young to be considering it, let alone with a girl who will one day transform into a vampire. I fear that you do not know what you are getting yourself into."

"Two days, Friar. That's all we have left until she turns." Romeo's voice cracked with emotion. "That is why we cannot delay. I want our union to occur while we are both human. And I know what I am facing. I am prepared to endure the hardships we might encounter, and I do not fear being ostracized. Please, Friar, do not deny us. I beg you."

Friar Laurence folded his hands in front of his chest and briefly bowed his head in meditation. When he was through, he grinned at Romeo as though he'd never had a doubt.

"You are an inspiration, Romeo," the friar said. "If everyone could love their enemy, just as you have, there would be peace on earth, I know it."

Romeo flushed a little at the friar's compliment. "Does that mean you will help us?"

"You and Juliet must meet me in my private cell

no later than three o'clock. And make sure you put on something that is fitting for a bridegroom. 'Tis your wedding, after all."

Romeo was so elated that he gave Friar Laurence a big hug. "A thousand thank-yous, my friend."

"You're welcome," the friar replied. "Perhaps this will turn your household's rancor to pure love."

Romeo smiled, his eyes twinkling with optimism. "Anything is possible."

After spending the morning coordinating the wedding ceremony with the friar, Romeo made his way toward the Montague homestead. As he trudged through the thick forest that separated the town from the low valley upon which the monastery was built, a fear began to take hold of him.

With Friar Laurence's gentle warnings still lingering in his ears, Romeo realized that his actions below Juliet's balcony had been extremely hasty. He truly wanted Juliet's hand in marriage, but now he was concerned that Juliet might have thought twice about his proposal. What if she thought he was a naive, lovesick fool and no longer took him seriously?

He felt remarkably uneasy for a man who was hours away from marrying the love of his life.

Romeo's eyes were on his feet as he kicked at loose pebbles in the road that led to his house. He was only ten steps away from the front door when an arrow whizzed by his head and struck the trunk of a tree. Romeo leaped behind a hedge in case another speeding arrow was on the way, his breath coming in swift spurts. But his panic turned to annoyance when he heard the familiar sound of rowdy laughter coming from the other side of the hedge.

When he stood up, he was eye to eye with Mercutio and Benvolio. His good friend was clapping his hands in amusement while his cousin held a bow up in the air, exclaiming, "Welcome home, Romeo!"

Romeo scowled. "Why can't you just wave hello like a normal person?"

"Because that wouldn't be any fun, would it?" Benvolio replied, poking Romeo hard in the shoulder.

"Speaking of fun, I can't help but wonder what happened with Romeo and the half-breed," Mercutio said, chuckling. Romeo wiped off his trousers and started walking toward the house, ignoring his friend's taunting, but clenching his hands into fists nonetheless.

Benvolio trailed close behind him, snickering in Romeo's ear. "Tell us how Rosaline was. We're dying to hear all the gory specifics."

Romeo continued to pretend that these words weren't eating away at him, knowing that the whole point of this teasing was to get him to react. But really, each taunt was like a punch to his gut.

"Oh, no. The sound of silence!" Mercutio caught up to them, still laughing.

"My guess is that their tryst did not go so well," Benvolio said in mock sympathy.

"Was she as cold as a corpse?" Mercutio asked, checking Romeo with his right hip.

Benvolio jabbed Romeo with his elbow. "Or wild as a banshee?"

Without any warning, Romeo swiveled around, locked his legs, and slammed his fist into Benvolio's jaw, sending him flying and tumbling to the ground. As Mercutio stood there, stunned, Romeo rammed his knee into his abdomen, causing him to squawk and fall flat on his face. Romeo stepped back and surveyed the damage, rubbing the back of his swelling hand.

"Sorry, good fellows. I don't know what came over me," he said sarcastically.

Mercutio coughed, then rolled over on his back. "No apologies necessary, Romeo."

"Yes, maybe we went a little over the line." Benvolio rubbed at his cheek.

"Maybe?" Romeo snapped.

"And I suppose you could have done without that brush with the arrow, too." Mercutio struggled to get up, but once he did, he grinned at Romeo.

Romeo willed himself to stay indignant, but as usual, when it came to Benvolio and Mercutio, he was unable to hold grudges against them for more than a few minutes. Maybe it was their willingness to protect him—as they'd done with Tybalt the night before—that softened his heart at irritating moments such as these.

"Let's just call it even and shake on it, okay?" Mercutio asked, holding out his hand.

Romeo nodded and smiled in agreement, but when Mercutio got a hold of his friend's hand, he twisted and bent it back so hard that Romeo actually screamed in pain.

"You dirty, slimy, no-good bastard!" he shouted.

"Don't blame me because you're so gullible," Mercutio said after letting go.

"Settle down, someone is coming up the path," Benvolio instructed as he stood up and straightened his shirt.

Romeo looked down the road while massaging his hand. Although he had only seen her face briefly last evening, he recognized the woman as Juliet's nurse. She was wrapped up in a heavy hand-knit yellow shawl and wearing a white bonnet that covered her light brown hair.

"Who is that?" Mercutio asked.

"None of your business," Romeo replied.

"Well, now I'm very curious," Benvolio said, smirking. "Mercutio, should I get out my bow and give her a special welcome?"

Romeo shoved Benvolio. "Get out of here, both of you. Or you will be sorrier than you were a moment ago."

Mercutio patted Benvolio on the back. "Come on, we've tortured him enough for today."

"Oh, fine," Benvolio said, disappointed.

Mercutio and Benvolio retreated into the house as the nurse approached. Romeo was practically bouncing on his heels with both anxiety and excitement. He inhaled slowly and told himself to have faith. Time apart, long distances, whatever the obstacle—together, he and Juliet had the power to overcome it.

"Greetings, Nurse. How are you this morning?" Romeo bowed in front of her as if she were a woman of royalty. It made all the sense in the world to get into her good graces.

The nurse wrung her hands nervously. "The time I have with you is short, Romeo. 'Tis almost the afternoon, and I have been gone from the castle for longer than expected."

"I understand," he said, swallowing hard. "Is Juliet still . . . I mean, will she—"

"My lady's only wish is to marry you, sir." The nurse glanced over her shoulders and kept her voice low. "But the clock is ticking, as you well know. And if anyone finds out about your impending union, the Capulets will try to kill you, and the prince's declaration of peace is certain to fall. God save our souls after that."

Romeo ignored almost everything the nurse had just said, except for two words: "marry you." In his excitement, he planted a kiss on each of the nurse's cheeks.

"Bless you, Nurse! You must tell Juliet to meet me at the monastery no later than three o'clock. Friar Laurence will perform the ceremony in his private cell."

The nurse took the edge of her apron and wiped off her cheeks. "A wedding without any witnesses? That is not what I had imagined for my dear Juliet."

Romeo sighed. "It is the best I can do right now."

"And what about later?" The nurse fiddled with a stray strand of yarn dangling from her shawl. "Where will you go after the wedding? Have you even thought that far?"

The nurse was right—Romeo hadn't considered that yet, and he should have. Once word got out, he and Juliet would be in too much danger in Transylvania. In fact, they might need to leave the province of Wallachia altogether. But admitting to the nurse that he had no plan would be a big mistake. She would tell Juliet about his lack of foresight for sure. He had no choice but to improvise.

"I have found a home for us in Moldova," Romeo lied. "We can go there after she has transitioned, when her parents will be less watchful of her."

The nurse glowered at him, doubt filling her narrowing eyes. "Do you know how to raise livestock?"

Romeo sighed again. "Why is that important?"

"Just answer the question, sir."

"No, but I am a quick learner," he replied.

"Juliet is going to need a steady diet of animal blood. If you are not able to raise livestock, your wife will have to go out at night and hunt for it, like a mangy, wild dog! How does that image sit with you?" the nurse scolded, pointing an angry finger at him.

Romeo's palms were starting to sweat. "It doesn't sit with me at all, madam. You must believe me when I tell you that I will do whatever it takes to—"

"You are just a boy!" The nurse's voice was now high-pitched and shrill. "And tomorrow at midnight Juliet is going to become a vampire. She will no longer be able to see the light of day. She will live forever with the hunger for human flesh gnawing at her gut. She will—"

"I know!" Romeo shouted, so loudly he made the nurse flinch. Then he took a deep breath and continued calmly. "What you are failing to understand is that none of that changes how I feel about her. And mark my words, nothing ever will."

"Nothing, eh? What about Juliet's initiation rite?" the nurse asked.

Romeo was completely confused. He had never heard of any initiation rite for vampires. "I do not know what you are talking about."

The nurse momentarily put her hand on her chest, and then shook her head while taking a step backward. "I must be going. I will give Juliet your message."

"Wait, this initiation rite—what is it? Why should it

concern me?" Romeo could sense that the nurse was hiding something from him.

"Never mind, I should have kept quiet about everything." The nurse turned around and headed down the path.

Romeo chased after her, though. Luckily, the nurse wasn't very fast because of her round size, so he was able to catch up to her. He halted right in front of the nurse, causing her to nearly trip over her own feet.

"If there is something else I should know about Juliet, please tell me," he said.

Tears formed at the inside corners of the nurse's eyes, then rolled down the sides of her short, upturned nose.

"She belongs with her family," she said simply, before pushing Romeo to the side and briskly walking away.

CHAPTER ELEVEN

s the rest of the house slept, Juliet paced back and forth in the castle's orchard, waiting for her nurse to return from town. She had been praying for good news from Romeo ever since a tiny killdeer bird had whistled outside her window, just a few minutes after daybreak. Now Juliet's eyes were set on the sun clock located in between two spruce trees. Although her nurse had left an hour ago, it felt as though she'd been gone for almost a year.

Juliet wrapped her arms around her middle, trying to prevent herself from coming apart at the seams. She turned her back to the sun clock and ambled over to a small fountain that was at the base of a marble statue of Vlad the Impaler. Juliet picked up the bottom of her pale pink dress and knelt down near the fountain, leaning over a bit so that she could see her reflection rippling in the water.

What she saw made her gasp in horror—her eyes had already lost their blue hue in favor of a deep shade of cherry red. Suddenly ten knots formed in Juliet's stomach, and she covered her mouth with both her hands to prevent herself from throwing up. But that only intensified her sickness. Juliet stared at her hands and watched in terror as her fingernails grew long and thick, just like her mother's and father's.

Juliet bowed her head and cried. While Romeo had said that he did not care that she was turning into a vampire, she worried that when he saw her like this, he would run away and never look back. She could not blame him—not after all of the pain and suffering vampires had caused the Montagues. But she couldn't help but think that death might be preferable to living forever, knowing that her greatest love had rejected her.

The sound of a squeaking fence hinge shook Juliet from her brooding.

"Who goes there?" she asked.

Out from behind a patch of small plum trees came her nurse. Juliet leaped up from the ground and sprinted over to her as fast as she could.

"I am so happy you are back!" she shouted, throwing her arms around the nurse and hugging her.

"Shh, child. You'll wake the undead." The nurse

kissed Juliet on the forehead and released her from their embrace.

"What can you tell me about my sweet Romeo?" Juliet said, her heart leaping inside her chest.

The nurse's eyes glazed over with tears as she looked at Juliet's red irises.

"It is all happening so fast," she muttered.

"Which is why you must help bring Romeo and me together." Juliet grabbed hold of the nurse's hand, careful that she didn't scratch it and draw blood. Lord knows how tempted she might be to taste it, now that her physical changes had begun.

The nurse squeezed Juliet's hand affectionately. "That will not stop the transition, my lady."

"That is exactly the reason I sent you to see him," Juliet said, her tone impatient. "Did he say again that he would love me now as a human, and later as a vampire? If he has changed his mind and heart, you can start digging my grave."

The nurse sighed heavily. "My lady, his loyalty and love for you expands with each breath he takes. He reassured me that nothing could ever keep him from you, not even your transformation, and he wants you to meet him at the friar's cell so that you two can be married."

Juliet clasped her hands together and glanced up to the sky. "Oh, how wonderful it is to hear those words!"

"Yes, they are wonderful words," the nurse replied.

"But he does not know the whole truth about you."

Juliet's smile began to fade away at this remark. "Indeed he does. I have told him everything."

"Everything except for your initiation rite," the nurse countered. "Don't you think your future husband should know that you will die on your sixteenth birthday unless you murder someone and drain them of all their blood?"

Juliet bowed her head and said nothing.

"And what about the fact that you are already engaged to be married?" the nurse added.

"Aren't there enough gruesome facts about me for him to accept? I cannot possibly—"

"Then why don't you just marry Count Paris?" the nurse interrupted, hugging Juliet and rocking her back and forth. "You have nothing to hide from him. You are one and the same, and your family will approve of your union. Why put yourself through this hell?"

"My eyes may have changed color, Nurse, but that does not make me blind," Juliet snapped, wiggling away from her. "Count Paris is not like me in the slightest, and my family only approves of him because they want to preserve their power. Honestly, Romeo Montague is more like my kin than any Capulet—he detests the violence between our families as much as I do. You will see, when he and I become joined, our hell will become our heaven."

"If heaven is where you want to reside with this

man, then you must not keep secrets from him," the nurse warned. "You must tell him the truth."

"I understand." Juliet gently took the nurse's shawl and put it over her own head. "Everyone here is still sleeping, and I must get to the friar's. Will you help sneak me out of the castle? Please?"

"It is against my better judgment, but I know you will do what you want anyway and I won't be able to stop you."

The nurse glanced around the orchard and found some beautiful white dog roses in a nearby bush. She grabbed some by the stem, ripped them free, and then handed them to Juliet.

"Here, a bride should not be without flowers on her wedding day," she said, wiping streams of tears from her face. "Now let us go, before I change my mind."

At around a quarter to three, Juliet and her nurse were at the monastery door, waiting to gain entrance. They had successfully evaded the guards at Capulet Castle by escaping through the tunnel system. The nurse had also led her through the forest and into the valley, using several unmarked paths.

Now that Juliet was on Friar Laurence's doorstep, her mind had been wiped clean of the entire journey. She no longer recalled the frantic race through trees, or her dress getting caught on prickly shrubs, which tore small holes in the fabric. She did not remember how the roots of her hair had become damp, although it was surely due to the condensation in the castle tunnels, or why her body ached all over, or where she had dropped her bouquet of flowers. But memory was no longer important to her. Everything that had happened in her life up until now seemed trivial and meaningless.

With the exception of meeting Romeo, of course.

As the nurse knocked on the door for the second time, Juliet felt a blinding pain pinch her stomach that caused her legs to wobble.

"Ugh, where is this man? We cannot stand out here forever. What if we are discovered?" the nurse complained as she knocked once again.

"By who? This monastery is not exactly a popular spot in Transylvania," Juliet replied.

The nurse turned to Juliet, a streak of moisture glistening on her top lip. "Perhaps one of the Montagues has gotten wind of this. They may have plotted to disrupt this wedding and chop your pretty head off!"

Juliet was surprised to find herself laughing. This wasn't out of the realm of possibility, but still, the thought of it was just so . . . comical.

"Do you actually think I'm trying to be funny?" the nurse asked, visibly irritated.

"No, I don't." Juliet fanned her face with her hands in an attempt to compose herself. "But it seems rather obvious that you think this wedding of mine will soon lead to my funeral."

The nurse lowered her head, her mood now somber. "Yes, and that is why I must remain out here."

"What? You are not going to give me away?" Juliet felt a ball of sadness building inside of her chest.

"Even though I wish this wasn't true, you are not mine to give, my lady," the nurse replied.

Juliet wanted to plead with her, but before she could, the door of the monastery opened. A thin, humble-looking, white-haired man in a brown robe appeared in the archway, smiling warmly as he bowed.

"Welcome, Juliet," he said. "Good tidings to you and your nurse."

"Hello, Friar." Juliet was thankful he had not greeted her with an awkward stare, for her appearance was not particularly bridelike. While there was no way to hide her demonic eyes, she crossed her arms in front of her chest so that he would not see her hands.

"This way, my lady." The friar held out his arm, just as a dutiful escort would. "Romeo awaits your presence in my private cell."

Juliet took his arm, but glanced over her shoulder, gazing longingly at her nurse. "You promise to wait for me?"

The nurse nodded and squeezed Juliet's shoulder affectionately.

Once Juliet was inside the monastery, her nervousness began to escalate. Although she wanted nothing more than to be with Romeo forever, there were so many unfamiliar and distressing urges crawling up and down her nearly snow white skin. As the friar led her through winding halls and countless rooms, she noticed that he had a small cut on his chin—most likely a scrape from shaving. But Juliet did not see this with her eyes.

She could smell his blood, even though it was drying.

The aroma was so distinct—like the scent of meat cooking on an open fire—and contact with it was beginning to intoxicate her. She could feel her mouth watering, and her head becoming light. She was using every ounce of willpower she had to steer her mind's focus where it belonged—on the eternal commitment she was about to make to Romeo Montague.

"Here we are, Juliet," the friar said, stopping in front of a door that wasn't much taller than he himself. "Are you ready?"

Regardless of the burgeoning love in her heart, Juliet could barely tear her eyes away from the friar's chin. Thankfully, she was able to shake herself out of her trance and nod.

The friar opened the door slowly and Juliet was met with the glorious glow of hundreds of purple candles, nestled firmly in waist-high cast-iron candlesticks. The windows were cracked open, and the breeze from outside sent the curtains billowing. There was a long, silken, silver carpet leading to an altar at the far end of the room, which was covered with cream lace cloth. Standing by that altar, dressed in a dark blue velveteen jacket, his hair neatly combed and a red rose in his hand, was Romeo.

Juliet wanted to sprint across the room and hold him in her arms. From the gigantic grin on Romeo's face, it seemed as though he wanted to do the same. Juliet was so enraptured that she felt like she was flying through the heavens like an angel.

But then Juliet saw a shadow fall over Romeo's eyes and watched his mouth drop open in shock.

"Juliet," he said in disbelief.

She thought Romeo might have been taken aback by her newly red eyes, but when the friar let go of her arm slowly and stepped away to gape at her in awe, she knew something else was horribly amiss.

"What's wrong?" Juliet said frantically.

Romeo gestured to her feet. Juliet looked down and saw that her delicate beige high heels were hovering six inches above the ground.

"Oh my God," she said, and gasped.

When her knees buckled and it seemed like she might crash to the floor, Romeo took off running, letting the rose flutter down to the carpet. But instead of barreling out the door, as Juliet suspected he might, he rushed to her side, catching her limp body in his arms. Juliet could not stop herself from sobbing, and Romeo cradled her until there were no more tears left for her to cry.

Despite the strange appearance of her clawlike fingernails, Juliet ran one of her hands through Romeo's hair, which felt just as she had expected it to—soft as goose down. As she stared at him, her worries about their future slowly began to dissolve.

Romeo gently pressed his forehead against hers, gazing deep into her flaming eyes. Juliet saw no doubt reflected back at her, or fear or futility. All that existed was the sparkle of unadulterated happiness.

In this moment, Juliet was neither human nor a vampire. She was an angelic spirit, soaring on the wings of true love.

"I don't think I can wait for the friar to marry us before I kiss you," Romeo whispered into her ear.

"Neither can I," she replied.

When Romeo kissed her for the very first time, Juliet thought his lips tasted like the finest powdered sugar. They were also unbelievably soft, just like tulip petals in early spring. The feeling that was stirring inside of her was like nothing she had ever known. It was as though her soul had been asleep for hundreds of years, and was now slowly waking up to a world that was made entirely out of sunlight.

The friar cleared his throat rather loudly. Romeo pulled himself away from Juliet, the glint in his eyes suggesting that it took every ounce of his energy to do so.

"Shall we proceed with the ceremony?" Friar Laurence asked, waving his hand toward the altar.

Juliet didn't hesitate with her answer. "Yes, Friar. I want this more than anything."

Romeo buried his face in her shoulder for a brief moment, and when he raised his head, Juliet noticed that his eyes were filling with tears of joy.

"I'm going to make you the happiest woman on earth," he whispered into her ear. "I promise."

"Come to the altar, both of you," Friar Laurence instructed.

Romeo set Juliet back down, though her feet no longer touched the floor. Now that she was floating above the ground, she was a good inch taller than he, but she could not worry about a trivial thing like that anymore. She had more important matters on her mind, like getting through the ceremony without being in physical pain. However, when Romeo took her hand and led her toward the altar, she realized that as long as she was close to him, not one part of her body ached.

Perhaps their love was more powerful than she thought.

"Please turn and face each other," Friar Laurence said as he picked up a large leather-bound book with bronze-foiled cursive letters engraved into the cover.

He flipped to the middle and then held the volume steadily in front of him.

Juliet turned to Romeo, pressing the palms of her hands onto his so that she would not scratch him with her nails. She kept her gaze focused on the warmth in his brown eyes.

"We are gathered together here in the sight of God to join together this man and this woman in holy matrimony," Friar Laurence read, his strong, reverent voice carrying throughout the room.

Juliet smiled when she felt Romeo tracing letters out on her right palm.

The first was the letter *F*. The second, *O*.

"If either of you know of any reason why you may not be lawfully joined together in matrimony, you must confess it."

The third letter was *R*. The fourth, *E*.

"If you do not confess, then you both are not joined together by God, and your marriage will not be lawful."

The fifth letter was *V*. The sixth, *E*. And the last was *R*.

Forever.

"Romeo Montague, will you take Juliet Capulet to be your wedded wife? Will you love her, comfort her, honor, and keep her, in sickness and in health, and forsaking all others, keeping only unto her, so long as you both shall live?" the friar asked.

Juliet gently squeezed Romeo's hands when she heard him reply, "I will."

The friar went on. "Juliet Capulet, will you take Romeo Montague to be your wedded husband? Will you love him, comfort him, honor, and keep him, in sickness and in health, and forsaking all others, keeping only unto him, so long as you both shall live?"

"I will," she proclaimed, then giggled when Romeo winked at her.

"Romeo, you must repeat after me," Friar Laurence said. "I, Romeo, take you, Juliet, as my wedded wife, to have and to hold from this day forward, for better for worse, for richer for poorer, in sickness and in health, to love and to cherish, till death do us part."

As Romeo repeated this sacred vow, Juliet could not stop herself from fixating on the friar's reference to death. A few days ago, she was considering suicide in order to avoid becoming a vampire. But now here she was, standing in front of a wonderful man, wanting desperately to live each and every day with him, regardless of whatever might happen to her body, mind, and soul.

Then in an instant, Juliet felt her stomach tie up in hundreds of tiny knots at the thought of Romeo dying. She knew it was twisted of her to be obsessing over such things at a magical time like this, but if she were being honest with herself, she had to accept the truth—immortal or not, she would not be able to go on without him.

"Now it is your turn, Juliet. Please repeat after me," said the friar. "I, Juliet, take you, Romeo, as my wedded husband, to have and to hold from this day forward, for better for worse, for richer for poorer, in sickness and in health, to love and to cherish, till death do us part."

Juliet composed herself and thought only of her love for Romeo. Then she repeated the vow with all of her conviction.

Friar Laurence leaned toward Romeo and asked, "Do you have any rings?"

Juliet watched as the twinkle in Romeo's eyes dimmed significantly. Then he caressed her hands gently.

"I'm sorry, my sweet, but I forgot to get them," he muttered in sheer embarrassment.

"That's all right," Juliet said softly. "Since we have to keep this marriage a secret, it's probably best that we do not wear rings."

Friar Laurence nodded in agreement. "You make a good point, Juliet."

Romeo sighed in relief and mouthed the words "thank you" to her.

"Now will you both please bow your heads?" the friar asked.

Juliet's heart swelled with blissfulness as she and Romeo heeded the friar's request.

"Eternal God, may Romeo and Juliet keep the vow they made, and may ever hereafter remain in perfect love and peace together, and live according to your laws."

Juliet was so anxious to lift her head and look into Romeo's eyes again, but this time as his spouse. She could barely contain her glee.

"I now pronounce you man and wife," said the friar.

"Can we look up now?" Romeo asked all of a sudden.

Juliet laughed.

"Yes, please do," Friar Laurence replied, closing his prayer book and grinning. "Romeo, you may kiss your bride."

Juliet's skin was ravaged by chills as Romeo trailed his hands up her arms and then down her back until he reached her waist. He stepped toward her and tilted his head up to accommodate Juliet's new height. When she put her hands on Romeo's shoulders, he pulled her very close to him so that their chests were lightly pressed together. Juliet leaned her face toward Romeo's until their lips touched tenderly.

Romeo's mouth was still as soft as tulip petals, but Juliet was quite alarmed that he no longer just tasted of sugar. This time, she swore she could somehow taste a hint of his Montague blood.

CHAPTER TWELVE

Romeo darted through the thick woods that surrounded the monastery, his boots flattening fallen autumn leaves as he ran. He ducked under looming tree branches and leaped over exposed, bulbous roots, laughing when he would occasionally trip and stumble.

Although his wedding day had been tinged with drama—he had certainly never expected his fiancée to start levitating before the ceremony—Romeo was brimming with vigor and exhilaration. The woman he loved so much had vowed to be his alone, and he had made that vow in return. All they had to do was wait for Juliet's sixteenth birthday to pass—then he could help her escape from Capulet Castle and the world would be theirs to explore, together.

Romeo arrived at the outskirts of town just before

twilight. The sky was dark indigo and gray clouds were scattered above him haphazardly. When he reached the cobblestone road that ran through the center of town, Romeo was panting, the cold air upon his cheeks making his skin raw. He was so overjoyed that he was afraid he'd have a terrible time hiding his secret wedding from Benvolio and Mercutio, who he was meeting at the village pub.

However, when Romeo saw that they were lingering outside the pub's front door, holding large metal steins in their hands, his worry disappeared. His cousin and friend probably would be more interested in drinking with the locals than prying into Romeo's personal life.

"Romeo, there you are!" Benvolio cried out, raising his stein in the air.

"Where have you been?" Mercutio asked. "We have been waiting for more than an hour."

Romeo patted his friend on the back and smiled. "Sorry I'm late. I was helping Friar Laurence repair something at the monastery. What did I miss?"

"Well, we plan to break our last drinking record by three glasses of ale at least." Benvolio smirked.

"That's ambitious. I doubt I'll be able to keep up with you." Romeo chuckled.

"Actually, gentlemen, it seems our fun for the night is already over," Mercutio grumbled while narrowing his eyes and looking over Romeo's shoulder.

Benvolio angrily chucked his stein to the ground, the contents pouring out into the street and streaming along the mortar between the stones.

"Actually, Mercutio, I feel that the fun has only just begun," he snarled.

Romeo was confused by this sudden change in their attitude—until he spun around and saw three humongous figures, dressed in all black, hovering over the ground not more than a few feet away. Their eyes were as red as Juliet's when Romeo kissed her on Friar Laurence's altar. Their sharp, pointy fangs were bared, an unmistakable indication that these vampires were ready to feed.

In the center of the trio was Tybalt, who snarled loudly as he floated toward Romeo. The vampire's brow was slick with sweat, and strands of his hair were coming loose from the tie at the back of his neck.

As he closed in, Romeo heard the sound of Mercutio drawing his sword from his sheath. He turned to his friend and shook his head, warning Mercutio not to do anything rash.

"Romeo Montague, you putrescent piece of scum," Tybalt crowed, puffing his broad chest out and pointing at him accusingly. "We have a score to settle!"

Even though Tybalt was the most intimidating vampire Romeo had ever encountered, he tried not to flinch in front of him. Instead he decided to try to defuse the tension like he'd done at the Capulet ball.

True, Tybalt had not found Romeo's antics amusing then, but maybe now it might work.

"Yes, I suppose we do," Romeo said cheerily. "Shall we go inside the pub and see who can drink the most without vomiting? It is a Montague score-settling tradition. Isn't it, men?"

Both Benvolio and Mercutio just sneered at the enemy.

As for Tybalt, his mood was not lightened in the least. He craned his head back and let out an ear-splitting wolflike howl that shattered a glass-plate window right behind Benvolio. Shards flew in every direction.

"I take it that is a no, then," Romeo mumbled.

"You shamed me in front of my uncle and the prince of Wallachia, and you defiled my entire family by setting foot on Capulet soil!" Tybalt shoved Romeo to the ground. "Get up, weakling, so I can fight you to the death."

"Charge after him, Romeo!" prompted Benvolio.

"Yes, show this bloodsucking ogre who the weakling really is," Mercutio encouraged.

Romeo stood up and dusted himself off. He knew that he could not do anything in retaliation. Tybalt was Juliet's cousin—harming him would mean hurting the woman Romeo adored. Also, the prince's treaty stated that anyone who violated its conditions would be executed. Perhaps if Romeo reminded Tybalt of these harsh consequences, he might back off.

"Have all of you forgotten about the treaty? If we defy Radu's law, we will face a death sentence," Romeo said urgently. "That goes for vampires, too."

"Tasting your blood in my mouth would be worth the punishment!" Tybalt shouted. He laughed and stuck out his large, veiny tongue while his cohorts snickered along with him.

The yelling must have carried in through the pub's windows, because a crowd was beginning to gather in the streets. Romeo's pulse raced as he saw several merchants and their customers circle around the feud. He had to ratchet down the tension here before it was too late.

"If you want to fight me, go ahead," Romeo blurted out. "But I will not throw one punch, nor will I swipe at you with a sword. There won't be much honor in that kind of kill, will there, Tybalt?"

The vampire considered Romeo's words for a moment and then broke into a sinister grin, nodding at his two henchmen to stand aside.

"Have it your way, coward," he grunted. "I will destroy you."

Just as Tybalt was about to advance on Romeo, Mercutio dove in front of his friend, his long-sword drawn and his eyes filled with hatred.

"You demon bastard!" he shouted. "I accept your challenge on Romeo's behalf!"

Romeo shoved Mercutio out of the way. "Stop this now. You don't need to get involved."

"We've been involved with these monsters for *years*, Cousin," Benvolio said.

"That's right. And surrendering to them is not an option, regardless of what the treaty says!" Mercutio exclaimed.

"Please, listen to me, friend. You don't have to do this," Romeo said, his voice wavering.

"You have never been on the battlefield." Mercutio stormed in front of Tybalt, his sword raised. "Now let me skin this beast and add his hide to the Montague collection."

Suddenly the vampire reeled his muscular arm back and thrust his large hand forward with all of his might, knocking Mercutio to the ground and slicing his cheek from his ear to his nose.

"I am going to eat you alive," Tybalt barked.

"Leave him alone, Tybalt!" Romeo shouted.

Before Romeo could put up more of a protest, Benvolio grabbed him from behind and put him in a stranglehold. Then he dragged a flailing Romeo, who was trying desperately to break free, off to the side with the rest of the onlookers.

"I won't allow you to ruin the Montague name," Benvolio said through gritted teeth.

Romeo attempted to kick at Benvolio, but when he did, Benvolio applied more pressure to his throat.

"Let me go—right now!" Romeo ordered, his face turning bright pink.

When Benvolio refused to respond, Romeo had no choice but to fix his eyes on Mercutio and Tybalt, who were circling each other in the street.

With blood running down his face and neck, Mercutio held on to his long-sword with two steady hands, the sharp end of the blade shining in the moonlight. Tybalt's arms were relaxed at his sides as he stared Mercutio down ruthlessly.

The vampire showed not one single ounce of fear, but Romeo was consumed by it. Like Benvolio had said, Romeo was considered too young to join in the family war against the Capulets. Watching them prepare for battle, Romeo struggled with the idea that at the end of this fight, someone would die.

And it would be his fault.

"Obliterate him, Mercutio!" Benvolio screamed.

This call to arms lit a fire in Mercutio, and with the loud bellow of a warrior, he charged at Tybalt with his sword raised above his head. Mercutio swiped at Tybalt with the speed of lightning, but Tybalt quickly flew out of the way. Mercutio's sword swung at Tybalt again, this time in an upward motion, which caught Tybalt off guard. Even so, Tybalt was too nimble, somersaulting backward like an acrobat. There were three more lashes from Mercutio's sword, none of them coming in contact with the vampire.

"Stop, Mercutio!" Romeo cried out as he took a large step back with his left leg. Using his center of gravity, he flipped Benvolio over his shoulder and broke away from his cousin's grasp.

Tybalt zoomed toward Mercutio just as Romeo broke through the crowd.

"Enough, Tybalt!" Romeo said as he came between Mercutio and their enemy.

"Get out of the way, Romeo," Mercutio urged, trying to see what his opponent was up to.

Tybalt's long cape flowed behind him like a shimmering beacon in the darkness. In less than a second, he soared over Romeo and landed behind Mercutio in time to dig deep into Mercutio's throat with his claws.

Romeo watched in horror as his friend gasped for air and blood seeped out of his mouth.

Mercutio dropped his sword to the ground. "Why, Romeo? Why did you come between us?"

"I—I just wanted to help," Romeo stammered.

"You should have left this alone," Mercutio choked.

"I'm so sorry, friend," Romeo said.

Mercutio took one final breath, and whispered his last words into Romeo's ear. "A plague on both your houses."

Then Tybalt snapped Mercutio's neck and crushed his windpipe in one fluid, masterful movement.

"No!" Romeo shrieked as Mercutio's eyes froze open. Amid a hundred horrified gasps, Tybalt pulled Mercutio's body away from Romeo and sank his teeth into Mercutio's jugular, sucking his prey's blood out, drop by drop.

Fueled by unbearable grief and anger, Romeo found a way to channel a brute power within himself and rip the vampire away from Mercutio's lifeless body.

Tybalt reeled backward, but managed to retain his balance. Mercutio's legs caved in underneath him, and Romeo tried to catch him by the arms. But Mercutio's weight was too much for him, so both of them toppled onto the cobblestone road. A distraught Romeo looked up at Tybalt, who was grinning at the gruesome scene before him.

"I had forgotten how delicious a feast like this can be," Tybalt said, licking his fingers. "I will remember to thank Mercutio when I see him in hell."

Romeo felt his skin turn hot like burning coals. Gone from his mind were thoughts of the treaty and the threat of execution and even Juliet's feelings. The rage building inside of him was explosive, and instead of trying to defuse it—as Romeo always had done—he surrendered to it, heart and soul.

Once he laid Mercutio on his back, Romeo shot up and faced Tybalt's blazing stare.

"You will be seeing my friend much sooner than you think," he threatened.

"Romeo! Take this!" yelled Benvolio, who had picked up Mercutio's long-sword. He tossed it in the air and Romeo caught the bronze handle with one hand.

Tybalt shook his head, chuckling. "You are no match for me."

"Why don't you come closer and find out for yourself?" Romeo taunted.

As Tybalt sized him up, Romeo begged the masters of providence to bless him. He laced his fingers around the sword's handle tightly, took a deep breath, and then waited for Tybalt to make the first move. If he watched his opponent carefully, he might be able to find a weak spot in his fighting technique.

"I said come closer, you dumb jackass!" he screamed, hoping to bait Tybalt with insults.

Romeo got precisely what he asked for. Instantly, Tybalt was careening toward him, his nostrils flaring. Romeo stood his ground. As soon as Tybalt was in range, he swept the sword forcefully in a lateral direction, the low end of the blade catching Tybalt on the hip.

"That was barely a scratch," he growled at Romeo as he took his knee and drove it into Romeo's gut.

Romeo coughed and blew out a few quick breaths, then Tybalt's elbow throttled down from above and jammed him right in the back. Romeo stumbled forward a few steps, but did not fall.

"You can do it, Cousin!" he heard Benvolio cheer.

Romeo regained his stature, but before he could reposition his long-sword, Tybalt was upon him once more. The vampire spun around in the air, leveling Romeo with a gargantuan kick to the skull.

Romeo's legs wobbled and suddenly he was flat on his back. Although he held on to the sword, he had taken such a wallop that he was momentarily blinded. It was as though God had extinguished all the stars in the universe and the world was covered in blackness.

Romeo could hear the crowd screaming now, the words overlapping each other in an incomprehensible, yet bone-chilling symphony of sound. Tybalt was coming for him—he knew it—but from where?

A demonic, deafening cry left the vampire's lips. Romeo could feel his steaming breath practically in his face and that was when instinct struck. While still lying on his back, Romeo used every shred of strength he had in his arms and sliced the long-sword through the air in a huge arcing motion.

Romeo heard two big thuds on the ground near him. And then there were exuberant shouts from the group of onlookers. Benvolio started shouting, "God save Romeo! God save Romeo!"

Romeo's eyesight came back soon after that, and the first thing that he saw was Tybalt's severed head, lying a foot away from his. He wanted to move but he was paralyzed with shock.

Benvolio was quick to pull his cousin up off the

ground. "You must run, Romeo. Hide with Friar Laurence."

"Oh, God, what have I done?" Romeo replied, covering his face with his bloodied hands.

A church bell sounded off in the distance, and the surrounding crowd began to scatter.

"Listen closely, Cousin." Benvolio shook Romeo by the shoulders to get his attention. "The bell means the prince and his men are in the town square. They should be here any moment. I will try to stave them off. But you must find a quick place to hide!"

Romeo spun around, his eyes darting frantically in different directions. He saw that the blacksmith's shop door was wide open. He sprinted toward the building, his heart caving in with each stride. Romeo ducked inside and locked the door behind him. Then he squatted behind a window, where no one could see him, and watched the calamity that was unfolding on the road.

With great haste, Benvolio enlisted some male citizens to dispose of Tybalt's body. The men had no trouble throwing the vampire corpse into a wheelbarrow, but none of them seemed eager to touch the severed head. After a lot of arguing, the townsmen dashed away with the wheelbarrow, leaving Tybalt's head where it lay.

Romeo closed his eyes for a minute and tried to catch his breath, but instead he suddenly became sick to his stomach. He knew the Montagues would want to keep the vampire's body as some kind of trophy—it was an honored family tradition that he thought was disgusting.

All of a sudden Romeo noticed that the bell had stopped ringing. He bowed his head and prayed that this nightmare would soon be over. But then he heard loud voices coming from the street. Romeo repositioned himself behind the window so he could get a clearer view.

Next to Benvolio and another townsman stood Prince Radu, dressed in a crisp, stately uniform. From the tense expressions on their faces, Romeo could tell that an ugly confrontation was only moments away. Off to the side was a small sampling of Radu's army— seven soldiers perched on black horses.

Romeo wiped beads of sweat from his forehead with his shirtsleeve. How would he be able to escape the consequences of what he'd done?

And then he spotted a noble female vampire, staring in horror at what was left of Tybalt. The more he stared at her, the more she bore a striking resemblance to Juliet.

Then it occurred to Romeo that this nightmare would *never* end.

"Which one of you vile humans killed my nephew?!" the woman said.

Now there was no doubt that this vampire was Romeo's mother-in-law, Lady Capulet. If she knew that

Romeo had secretly married her daughter and murdered her nephew, she might go on a wild rampage and kill everyone in sight.

"I demand to know what happened here." Prince Radu closed in on Benvolio, the expression on his face stern and intimidating.

Benvolio stood firmly and showed no fear. "The truth is that Romeo Montague is responsible for Tybalt's death."

Lady Capulet narrowed her flaming eyes at Benvolio and said, "Then tell us where he is, so we can execute him."

"I don't know his whereabouts, and even if I did, I wouldn't tell you," Benvolio snarled at the vampire. Then he pointed to Mercutio's pale, lifeless body.

"Your precious nephew challenged Romeo to a fight to the death, but Romeo was far too noble to accept! He wanted to respect the peace treaty and, for some strange reason, Tybalt's life," Benvolio explained. "Mercutio, on the other hand, could see in Tybalt's beady eyes that he was out for blood at any cost, so he accepted the vampire's challenge. Mercutio fought Tybalt valiantly, but Romeo interfered and tried to stop them. Tybalt could see that Mercutio was distracted and instead of backing off like a gentleman, he slaughtered Mercutio like a wild beast! If you ask me, Tybalt got exactly what he deserved."

Romeo could see from the ferocious look on Lady

Capulet's face that she was brimming with anger.

"I can smell your blood, sir." Lady Capulet poked Benvolio in the chest with a sharp fingernail. "You are a Montague. You will say and do anything to protect your kin. Everything that has come out of your mouth has been lies."

Romeo leaned closer to the glass of the blacksmith shop window, wishing there was some way to protect his cousin.

The prince looked to one of the townsmen, crossing his arms in front of his chest. "Were you a witness to this?"

The man stepped in between Benvolio and Lady Capulet, taking off his hat as a sign of respect.

"I was, Prince. And I swear on my mother's grave that what Benvolio has told you is true," the townsman said. "There were many others who saw the fight, too. I'm sure they would all say the same if you asked them."

Prince Radu was silent for a moment. "Nevertheless, Tybalt and Romeo are both in violation of the treaty."

"Yes, but Tybalt started this mess, Your Highness," Benvolio reasoned. "In my humble opinion, executing Romeo does not seem like a just punishment."

Romeo managed a weak smile. His cousin was going to such great lengths to save his life. How would he ever be able to repay Benvolio for his loyalty?

"Well, I have taken all the facts into consideration.

I'm sure that your cousin was devastated when he saw his friend killed right in front of him. Still, he broke the law, and I cannot.abide by that, regardless of the circumstances," Prince Radu said. "Therefore, I will have my men put up notices around town. Romeo Montague is hereby exiled from Transylvania and all of Wallachia."

"Pardon me, Your Highness, but what if he defies his sentence and refuses to leave?" Lady Capulet sounded completely exasperated. "The Montagues have plenty of allies here; they would certainly give Romeo sanctuary."

"If Romeo is found within the borders of Wallachia, then the original punishment of execution will be enforced. I'll put fifty men from my cavalry on patrol," Prince Radu proclaimed. "And anyone who provides him with a place to hide will face imprisonment."

"Thank you, sir," Lady Capulet said.

Soon after the prince made his declaration, he and Lady Capulet followed his cavalry out of the village. As for Benvolio and the townsman, they wandered over to Mercutio's body. Regardless of how many of Radu's soldiers could be lurking around any corner, Romeo could not bear the sight of his cousin preparing to bury his closest friend.

So he opened the front door and ran as fast as his legs could carry him.

CHAPTER THIRTEEN

Juliet always loved being in the orchard in the evening. Usually, the sweet smell of citrus and the sound of leaves rustling in the wind would carry through the evening air and relax her. But tonight was different from any other. Hour after hour, Juliet's body continued to undergo a slow metamorphosis, the hunger pains inside making her ravenous and almost crazed. She could only imagine how bad it was going to be tomorrow at midnight. However, she still could not fathom committing the act that would end this agony once and for all.

Juliet sat on a bench with her knees up to her chest, rocking back and forth to prevent herself from succumbing to anxiety. Although she was thankful to have returned to the castle without any of her relatives suspecting a thing, she was still a worried newlywed.

Tonight, she and Romeo should have been celebrating their marriage with a romantic honeymoon. But instead she was trapped—inside this wicked fortress, and within her own skin.

Romeo said they had to wait to escape, that it would be easier to disappear once she had finished her transformation. But her husband did not have all the facts. And he could not feel the intense physical anguish that Juliet was experiencing. Juliet shuddered as she remembered how deliriously happy Romeo was when they parted at the monastery. But how would he feel after tomorrow, when she became a full member of the undead?

"Miss Juliet! Miss Juliet!"

She looked up and saw her nurse galloping toward her with her arms raised in the air. Juliet could tell that something was wrong. She sprang up from the bench and greeted her nurse with a warm embrace.

"Has something happened to Romeo?" Juliet asked.

The nurse's breath was quick and shallow, her eyes filled with tears. "Yes, my child. I come to you with terrible news."

"Go on," Juliet said, clenching her jaw and bracing herself.

The nurse began to sob and wiped her nose with the sleeve of her blouse. "I don't know if I can bring myself to tell you this. You are in such a delicate state."

"My state is more dire than delicate. Now I must

know what happened," Juliet said, her voice tense and agitated.

"It is such a tragedy. Words are escaping me," the nurse whimpered.

All of a sudden a powerful bolt of anger ripped through Juliet.

"My patience is at an end!" She grabbed the nurse by the shoulders, shaking her so hard that the nurse's bonnet fell right off her head. "You must tell me what you know!"

"He is dead, my lady!" the nurse blurted out. "Gone from this earth forever."

Juliet dropped the nurse and crumbled to the ground. Her red eyes burned as tears formed, and all of her muscles became twisted like the vine of a rope.

"My husband is . . . dead?" she said in a faint whisper. "Now I despise God just as much as He despises me."

The nurse crouched down and lifted Juliet's chin up. "No, Juliet. Romeo is among the living. You should mourn for your cousin Tybalt."

Never before had Juliet felt such contradictory feelings at the exact same time. She was elated and overjoyed that her darling Romeo was safe, but devastated and sickened that Tybalt's immortal life had been cut drastically short.

"My heart has been torn in half," Juliet said, her hands trembling as she cried. "Please, tell me what happened."

The nurse wiped Juliet's tears away with her finger-tips. "Tybalt was killed in town during a street fight."

"I always told him to be careful with that temper of his," Juliet mumbled. "But he was never one to listen to reason."

"He was a stubborn young man," the nurse agreed. "And prideful, too. It's a volatile combination."

A flood of visions briefly resurfaced in Juliet's mind—memories of her and Tybalt swimming in the castle's pond and sneaking into the kitchen for late-night treats like honey cakes and yellow cheese; flashbacks of the first Montague raid, when Tybalt picked her up and carried her to safety from her chambers to one of the castle towers; the fine details of his face—his impish smile, rounded cheeks, and wide eyes that once glimmered blue—none of which she would ever see again.

Juliet bowed her head in sadness. "I hate the man who took my cousin away from me."

There was a long, unnerving silence, which the nurse broke with a sorrowful voice.

"Then you hate the man you married, my lady."

Juliet felt another angry, rumbling sensation in the pit of her stomach, and within moments, it spread throughout her body.

"Liar!" she shrieked. "Romeo would never do some-thing that evil and treacherous. He told me himself that he has never harmed another creature."

"He was provoked, madam. I went into town to do an errand and saw the clash firsthand, so did a crowd of witnesses," the nurse stated.

Juliet closed her crimson eyes and tried to regain power over her body and soul. After a few deep breaths, she said, "Tell me everything."

"Tybalt challenged Romeo to a duel, but your husband would not accept, in honor of the peace treaty. But then his friend Mercutio stepped in and battled Tybalt. After a lengthy fight, he overcame Mercutio and crushed the poor man's neck with his bare hands."

Juliet was slowly coming back to herself, the fury inside of her subsiding.

"After that, Tybalt tore into Mercutio's flesh with his teeth and drank the man's blood, right then and there." The nurse dabbed at her runny nose with the hem of her skirt. "Romeo went wild with grief and fought Tybalt to the death. Now your cousin's carcass is a trophy for the Montagues, and Romeo is exiled . . . he has vanished, my lady."

"Nurse, you have to find him!" Juliet said. She was so consumed with grief, she felt as though someone had put his hands around her neck and was trying to choke her.

"You are at your wits' end, madam. No. You must forget Romeo. He is just as dead as Tybalt as far as the government is concerned," the nurse said.

Juliet pounced on the nurse, taking her hand and

kissing it affectionately. "Oh, do not be vindictive, Nurse. I am so sorry for yelling at you—"

"I watched your cousin Tybalt go through the same changes," the nurse interjected. "So I do understand. It's difficult to control your impulses as you transition."

"Then why won't you do what I ask?"

"Because what you want is impossible to get. Romeo is banished. He has most likely traveled to the border of Moldova and crossed it. I cannot go after him."

Juliet knew that her nurse was wrong. This afternoon, she had pledged her undying loyalty to Romeo, and he did the same in return, with just as much passion. The bond between them was unbreakable, even more so than the one Juliet had with her precious nurse. She knew that no circumstances, no matter how extreme, could ever force him to betray their love, no matter what anyone else believed to be true.

"He is still here, I can feel it all over," Juliet said, slipping a turquoise ring off her right index finger. "Nurse, you must search for him at the monastery. Friar Laurence would certainly give him refuge. Then give this ring to my true knight, and bid him to come to the castle."

"I beg you to let this go, Juliet," the nurse implored. "You have other choices."

"None that will make me happy!" Juliet barked. Another uncontrollable angry fit was about to seize her. "I have one more day before the transition. If I am separated from Romeo, I will not survive it."

The nurse stood up and smoothed out her dress, then picked her bonnet off the ground and put it back on her head. Juliet saw that her nurse was near tears.

"I pray that you do, my child, because I don't know if I could survive without you."

CHAPTER FOURTEEN

omeo walked in circles within the confines of
Friar Laurence's cell, his hands and shirt still
covered in Tybalt's blood. His pulse was racing even
faster than it had when he ran from the outskirts of
town all the way to the monastery. Now he was trapped
between four walls and could do nothing but fixate on
the terrifying images of Mercutio's vicious murder and
Tybalt's butchered head lying in the dirt.

Romeo tried to release the tension in his neck by
tilting his head to the right and left, but it did not work.
He attempted to console himself with the thought of
Prince Radu's leniency toward him, but that brought
him no comfort either. Banishment would keep him
from his precious Juliet—for who knew how long—and
that would surely be torture.

He stopped pacing and stood in front of a stained-glass window in the friar's cell, leaning his forehead against the glass as he gazed out into the woods. His hands trembled at his side, and his lower lip quaked. The realization of what he had done—willfully taken someone's life—was fully sinking in.

Although Tybalt had instigated the fight, and Romeo's act of vengeance would probably be considered justified in the court of public opinion, he was drowning in guilt. If he hadn't trespassed at the Capulets' castle, none of this would have come to pass. But then he never would have met his soul mate.

. . . Who was also the cousin of the vampire he'd just slaughtered.

There was a knock on the door and Romeo's breath caught in his throat.

"It's only me." The friar's gentle voice echoed out in the hallway. "May I enter?"

Romeo sat down in a chair, sighing with relief. "Yes, of course."

Friar Laurence came in carrying a large wooden bucket full of water. He struggled to get it across the room, small streams of liquid splashing to the ground as he walked.

"Here, I hope this is enough to clean you up." Friar Laurence wiped a few beads of perspiration near his temples, then reached into his robe's left pocket and brought out a bar of light green soap. "This is made with olive oil, so it should get rid of the bloodstains on your skin. I am not sure about your clothes, though."

Romeo could barely look the friar in the eyes. "Thank you."

"You're welcome," Friar Laurence responded. "Shall I leave you now?"

"No, I would like the company. I just . . . I don't know what to say."

"You are in shock. Anyone would be," the friar said.

"Do you not know? We vampire-killing Montagues are made of steel," Romeo said.

He stared at the spatter of blood across his shirt-sleeves, which must have come from Tybalt. The large bloodstain in the center was from when he had held Mercutio in his arms as his friend took his dying breath. The more Romeo looked at his shirt, the more enraged he became. He tore the shirt into pieces, throwing the shreds on the floor.

Romeo knelt down next to the bucket and scooped up some water with both his hands. He poured it over his face three times, and then he broke down into silent sobs, his shoulders shaking.

"I am so sorry, Friar," he cried out. "I never meant for any of this to happen."

The friar placed a hand on top of Romeo's head. "If you ask for forgiveness, Son, it will be granted."

Romeo opened his eyes and watched his own image reflected in the water. The young man he saw there was completely unrecognizable. No longer was he a naive boy who daydreamed about love. Instead that boy was replaced by a man, who had come face-to-face with death, and lived to tell about it.

Only there was one person he never wanted to tell.

"You do not understand, Friar," Romeo lamented. "I have killed Juliet's cousin, who she loved deeply. When she hears of this, she will hate me, and without her, my entire world will turn to dust."

The friar pulled Romeo away from the bucket, sitting him on the floor and wrapping a towel around him. "You are not the Almighty, Romeo, which means you cannot predict the future. All you can do is pray."

"Pardon me, Friar, but praying will not end my banishment," Romeo said, shivering.

Friar Laurence was about to respond when the sound of pebbles hitting the stained-glass windows of the monastery distracted him. "Hurry, Romeo! Conceal yourself. Someone is here."

Romeo got up and scurried into the friar's closet, which was filled with cloaks and robes for church services. He pushed himself deep into the back so the fabric would keep him hidden, and he listened as the friar called out, "Who is it?" Romeo could not hear the reply, but when Friar Laurence said, "Yes, indeed. One moment, my lady," he had a wild hope that it was Juliet, coming to reunite with him so they could run away from Transylvania and never look back.

However, when the friar led him out of the cloak closet a few moments later, Romeo saw Juliet's nurse standing before him. Her puffy eyes and drooping mouth made it clear to him that she was aware of what happened—but did that mean Juliet knew as well?

"Nurse, please be quick," Romeo pleaded. "What news have you brought from my dearest love?"

"Juliet is eager to see you, sir, and requests your presence at the castle." The nurse's lips trembled nervously as she spoke.

Romeo glanced down at his red-stained hands. "Then I suppose she does not know about my fight with Tybalt."

"Juliet knows," the nurse stated, her voice laden with sadness. "Still, she yearns to be with her husband." She held out her hand and opened it, revealing a sparkling turquoise ring. "This is but a small token of her devotion. Will you heed her call and come to the castle?"

Tears of relief and happiness welled up in Romeo's eyes, but he could not quite believe what he was hearing. Did Juliet love him enough to overlook such an unthinkable sin as the cold-blooded murder of her own kinsman?

"She has forgiven you, Romeo, without you even having to ask. That is the purest love there is. Go to her," the friar urged.

"But I am a fugitive, and the Capulets know I am

the one who killed Tybalt. If they do not strike me down on the way to the castle, then the prince's army will."

The friar wandered over to large closet in the corner of the room and pulled out a white hooded robe with a gold rope belt. "I usually wear this when I go into town. If you put the hood up, most people will think you are me. Being in the nurse's company will help, too. I doubt you'll be approached by any soldier—human or vampire—while in her presence."

Romeo cracked a small smile. "Thank you, Friar."

"You must be aware of something, Romeo Montague," the nurse said, pointing a short, stubby finger at him. "Juliet's transformation into a vampire is nearly complete. I hope you are prepared to deal with all that it entails."

Romeo put his hand over his heart. "Juliet is my wife, now and forever. My love for her will never be swayed."

The nurse shook her head in dismay. "If neither of you will listen to reason, then God help you both."

The next morning, Romeo was lying on his side in Juliet's bed, watching her chest rise and fall as she slept. Her brown hair was fanned out on top of a pillow, her pale skin a stark contrast to the burgundy-colored satin sheets. Romeo did not want to disturb her, but he could not resist running one of his fingers down the length of her bare arm or planting a soft kiss on the back of her delicate neck.

His beautiful wife squirmed a little, but did not awaken, much to Romeo's relief. They had been up all night long. The moment the nurse had smuggled Romeo into Juliet's chambers and left them alone, their passions overtook them, so much so that the pain in Juliet's changing body seemed to disappear as they held each other. Romeo smiled happily as glimpses of those heavenly hours passed through his mind—the urgent kisses and gentle touches. He could not comprehend what he'd done in his life to deserve such a perfect creature.

A gust of wind banged a tree branch against the window of Juliet's room, startling Romeo. He checked on Juliet to see if she had been disturbed, but her eyes remained closed. Romeo slid out from underneath the sheets gingerly and placed his feet on the cool floor. Then he got up and stretched, raising his arms in the air and yawning. He walked over to the window and pulled the curtains open so light could filter into the dark room. Romeo stood there grinning, his chest and face now warm from the dawning sun.

But his quiet moment of contentment was broken by the sound of Juliet crying out in agony. Romeo spun around in surprise and found her sitting up in bed, squinting and holding her hands in front of her face.

"What is it, my love?" Romeo said, rushing over to her in a panic.

"The light! The light!" she replied, panting as though she had just awoken from a horrible dream. "Hurry, it burns!"

Romeo bounded back to the window. He yanked the heavy curtains closed and soon the room was as dark as night. Romeo chided himself for not remembering how the sun would affect his wife on this most significant day.

He turned back around to find her curled up in bed, sobbing. Romeo approached her slowly, his heart truly aching for her. He thought about what he might say to comfort her, but then realized that no words would bring his bride any peace, not even "I love you."

As he sat down on the edge of the bed, Juliet crawled over to him and burrowed her face into his bare shoulder. Romeo rubbed her back with the palm of his hand and repeatedly kissed the top of her head.

"I am so sorry," Juliet whimpered.

"Why are you apologizing? I am the one who is so absentminded," Romeo said. "I did not give opening those curtains a second thought."

Juliet sniffled. "That is exactly why I am sorry. You shouldn't have to think twice before doing such a simple thing."

"It will just take some getting used to," Romeo said, cuddling her tighter. "Try not to worry."

Juliet pressed her lips gently against his chest. "I fear that's all I can do."

"No, my sweet, it's not," Romeo murmured. "Look at me, Juliet."

Juliet raised her head a little so she could gaze upon him with ruby-colored eyes.

"Just for a moment, can we pretend that this bed is . . . an uncharted island?" Romeo said with a small grin. "Very small and secluded. No one will find us here."

From the smirk growing on Juliet's face, he could tell this game might actually lift her spirits. "Where is this island exactly?"

"Oh, off the coast of Persia," he continued. "It's quite warm, and the sand at the beach sparkles like gold."

"That sounds heavenly." Juliet placed a kiss on Romeo's cheek. "Can we smell the sea salt in the air?"

Romeo laid Juliet on her back, tucking a strand of her hair behind her ear. "Of course we can."

"What about food?" Juliet asked as she brought her hands behind Romeo's neck and laced her fingers with his.

"Food, yes, we will certainly need that," Romeo said, kissing the inside of her wrists. "What if I became a fisherman and you gathered nuts and berries?"

Juliet pulled Romeo toward her. The faint scent of

her perfume practically put him in a trance. "I don't think you are the fisherman type."

"Really? Why not?"

Juliet closed her eyes and sighed. "Because you aren't a killer . . . of any living thing."

Romeo's eyes widened, surprised by the realization that Juliet had not brought up his showdown with Tybalt since he'd arrived in her chambers. Now here she was, showing him that she believed he'd never set out to harm anyone. At this moment Romeo felt that Juliet knew him like no one else did.

"You're right, I'm not." Romeo kissed Juliet's lips as she ran her hands down his back.

"Tell me that we are never going to leave this island," Juliet murmured.

"I wish I could," Romeo replied with regret in his voice. "But we can pretend for a little while longer."

All of a sudden Juliet turned her head away from him, her lower lip trembling. "Wishes are the only thing we have right now, aren't they?"

Romeo's pulse quickened—he didn't want Juliet to become upset again.

"We have love. If we have that, everything will be fine," Romeo whispered, kissing her on the softest part of her neck.

"No, Romeo. It will not." Juliet wiggled out from Romeo's embrace, sat up against the dark wood headboard of her bed, and looked at him with her smoldering eyes. "I want to believe that our love will conquer all—truly I do—but perhaps we've been foolish. Now that you are exiled, our plans to escape together are almost impossible. And today, I become everything I detest."

Romeo tenderly laid a finger on Juliet's lips and silenced her. "Do not detest yourself for something you cannot control. And we will figure out a way to be together. I am sure of it. My dear, how can you question the strength of our love, after how you have forgiven me for what I did to Tybalt? In all my life, I have not known someone so selfless, courageous, and loving."

Now tears were streaming down Juliet's cheeks, one after the other. Romeo swallowed hard, fearing that his wife might be having second thoughts. He cupped her face in his hands, hoping to calm her.

Juliet shook her head. "The nurse explained how Tybalt started the awful fight. I loved my cousin, but if he had respected the law, you would not have broken it either."

Still Juliet wept, even harder than before. "But . . . but—"

"Are you concerned about whether I'll still love you as a vampire?" Romeo interjected.

Juliet managed a small nod.

"Darling, my love for you today is greater than it was for you yesterday, and I will be true to you. Always," Romeo said.

"But there is something important I have kept from you." Juliet's voice was as soft as the sheet that covered her body.

"Whatever it is, you can share it with me," Romeo said.

Juliet wiped at her cheeks with her hands. "I do not know where to begin."

Romeo leaned in and kissed her on the lips. "Just take a deep breath and the words will come."

Juliet did as he suggested and drew in a long breath, then let it out very slowly. She swallowed hard and began.

"There is an initiation rite that I have to perform by midnight," Juliet said in monotone.

Romeo's eyes flashed with recognition. "Yes, your nurse had said something about that, but she did not fully explain."

Juliet grinned a little. "She thought better of it, I suppose. She doesn't approve of our marriage, but she still wants me to be happy. And if she'd told you, well, who knows what would have happened."

"Why do you underestimate me, Juliet?" Romeo took her by the hands and kissed them.

"It's not that. It's—"

The door to her chamber flew open without warning. Romeo dove for his trousers, hitting his head on the bedpost, as Juliet covered herself by pulling the sheet up to her neck.

"Juliet!" her nurse proclaimed as she barged into the room.

Romeo had no time to be embarrassed as he threw on his clothes. He could see how distressed the nurse appeared—perhaps he and Juliet had overslept?

"Nurse! What is the matter?" Juliet asked.

"Maribel just came and told me. A few of the prince's men are at the castle to interrogate the servants about Romeo's presence at the ball. Apparently, the Capulets believe there are Montague sympathizers in our ranks." The nurse grabbed a robe from Juliet's closet and quickly handed it to her. "We must get him out of here."

Romeo finished getting dressed as the nurse tended to Juliet. After she put on her robe, Juliet embraced him.

"My lord, my love, my friend," she whispered into his ear. "Will you come back for me, despite the things you do not yet know?"

Romeo caressed the back of her neck. "I promise nothing will keep me away. Not even exile."

Finally, Juliet was able to smile. "Good-bye for now, Husband."

Romeo let Juliet go with great reluctance, and moved to the window overlooking the orchard. He would have to climb down the wall outside in order to escape.

"Wear this, sir. Just in case." The nurse handed

Romeo a wooden crucifix pendant on a long leather band. "Most everyone has gone to sleep in their chambers, but there may be a stray or two."

Romeo took the pendant and put it over his head. "But what about—"

"I tied the dogs up, sir," the nurse interrupted. "Now go, before the prince's men find you."

Romeo glanced at his precious Juliet, who was floating in front of him like an effervescent angel. "One kiss, and I'll descend."

Juliet placed her hands on the back of his head, their lips touching much too quickly. Then Romeo slid between the curtains and out into the sunlight, which his bride would never be able to see again.

CHAPTER FIFTEEN

s soon as the sun set, Lady Capulet barged into Juliet's chambers, with her hands placed firmly on her hips and her lips tightly pursed. She floated straight toward her daughter's secret marriage bed and began fluffing the pillows, one by one.

"I'm sorry to inform you of this on your birthday," she said matter-of-factly. "Tybalt was killed last evening. Prince Radu and I found his head in the street. How despicable."

Juliet stood at the foot of the bed, marveling at how unfeeling her mother seemed. How could she deliver such tragic news so casually—as though she were giving one of her servants a list of chores to tend to?

Lady Capulet glided over to Juliet, her eyebrows raised. Juliet tugged at the collar of her robe, closing it tightly so her mother could not see any of the pink love bites that Romeo had left on her skin.

"Do you have nothing to say about the loss of your cousin?" Lady Capulet asked.

Juliet did have something to say, but it was not about Tybalt. Even with moral corruption and starvation on the horizon, for a brief moment, she was tempted to tell her mother she had married Romeo.

How would her mother respond if she found out Juliet's husband was a Montague? Juliet knew that it would strike both her parents down like wooden stakes to their chests, but only after they killed her first.

Juliet had to do what she could to stay alive, so that she and Romeo could flee Transylvania together.

Which included tolerating her mother's insensitivity.

"The nurse told me about Tybalt's slaying," Juliet said, her tone downtrodden. "My dull mood must seem strange, but I think I'm in shock."

Lady Capulet examined Juliet from head to toe. "Now is not the time to grieve, Juliet. The last step in your transition is tonight, which means your life depends on the strength of all your senses."

Juliet had no energy left to combat her mother, so she just nodded dutifully.

Lady Capulet floated away from her daughter and sat down in a chair. She conjured up a folded fan out of thin air. Juliet flinched when it snapped open all by itself and began waving in front of her mother's unusually sallow face.

"Speaking of which, your father and I have talked about your distress over initiation," she said matter-of-factly. "I think we've come up with a solution that might make you feel more comfortable with it."

Juliet's mouth suddenly went dry. Had her mother and father actually found a way to spare her from cannibalizing some poor innocent person? Perhaps they were capable of some human decency once in a while. "Please, tell me."

"Tybalt was slain by that wretched son of Lord Montague," Lady Capulet said. "Thus, he is the perfect candidate for your first taste of blood. Don't you agree?"

If there had been any color left in Juliet's face, it would have faded from view that instant.

"You and Father want me to . . . murder Romeo Montague?" Juliet could not believe that those words had fallen off of her tongue.

"If you do not, another one of us will," her mother said. "There are plenty of Capulets who are out searching for him now, ready to snap him in two."

Juliet could not move a muscle. Her mouth hung agape and her breath caught in her throat.

"Why do you look so shocked?" Lady Capulet plucked the fan out of the air with her hand and whipped it shut. "You need to feed on human flesh by midnight and this man slaughtered your cousin. Our family deserves revenge!"

"Not at the expense of my soul!" Juliet shouted before doubling over in sidesplitting pain.

"Look at you! You are in anguish and still hiding behind your morals. Romeo is not some innocent villager, Juliet. He is guilty of murdering your cousin, he deserves to die," Lady Capulet said tersely.

"What gives you the right to decide what happens with people's lives?" Juliet snapped back through gritted teeth.

"Well, as your mother, I suppose I have the right to decide what happens with *you*," she said coldly.

Juliet redirected all the physical agony she was experiencing and transformed it into the courage to stand up for herself. "But I can decide whether or not to obey."

Lady Capulet leaned forward in her chair, her lips pressed together tightly. "I spoke to your father about postponing your marriage to Count Paris tomorrow, and he outright refused."

"Based on what grounds?!" Juliet yelled.

"Look at me, Juliet!" her mother shouted. "Are you oblivious to the changes happening right before your eyes?"

"You appear to be fine," Juliet replied.

Lady Capulet flew out of her chair, leaping at Juliet.

"I will not repeat myself again, Juliet. Look at me."

Juliet's hands trembled as she studied her mother. When she observed Lady Capulet this closely, she did notice some oddities. There were visible cracks in the skin on her face. The red glow of her eyes was dimmer than it had been the day before.

"So it is true," Juliet murmured as she touched one of the wrinkles on Lady Capulet's cheek. "Human blood is what gives vampires their power. But does this mean you are going to—"

"Die? No, we still have our immortality. But we are weaker and less able to protect all that is rightfully ours—this castle, the land, our riches, everything that we treasure. Which is why we need to put an end to this peace treaty," her mother insisted.

"I still don't understand how my marriage to Count Paris will help."

Lady Capulet sighed in frustration. "We suspect that Count Paris is turning women as a means of getting human blood. Once he drinks his fill from them, and they are given a taste of his own blood, they are transformed into vampires. And the more vampires there are, the more competition there is. Not for just food, but for status, power, and dominion over Transylvania."

Juliet's eyes flickered with recognition. She was right—her parents were out to preserve their empire, not just fighting for their physical survival. How selfish could they be?

"Your father believes that the count might change his ways if he settles down with a wife," Lady Capulet continued. "Then perhaps he will be more motivated to pressure Prince Radu to overturn the treaty. Now do you see how important your role is in all this?"

"But the fan—you conjured it here without any difficulty. Your powers can't be waning too badly. Maybe there's some other explanation, or maybe there is a way to stop your strength from deteriorating," Juliet said, her voice wavering.

"It would not be wise for you to pin your hopes on a parlor trick." Lady Capulet pushed Juliet's hand away with disdain. "The prosperity of the Capulets rests on your shoulders, Juliet. I will not allow you to turn your back on us."

"Perhaps there is something else the count wants." Juliet tried to negotiate. "Like money or jewels or property. I would give everything I have to him—just not my heart, or my life."

Lady Capulet responded to her daughter's pleas by floating out the door without another word.

Juliet breathed in deeply, trying to swallow the huge lump in her throat, and gripped one of the bedposts with both hands. She racked her brain for a way to stop her life from spiraling out of control any further, and nothing came to her.

Truly, there was no hope. No hope whatsoever.

"Are you decent, my lady?" came a voice from across the room.

Juliet glanced at the door, which was opened just a crack. The round pink face of her nurse peeked through.

"Decent? Hardly. But you may come in anyway," she answered solemnly.

The nurse came in carrying a large metal box with a long coiled handle made out of thick wire. She set it down on the desk opposite Juliet's bed and wiped off her hands with the bottom of her apron.

"What is that?" Juliet inquired.

The nurse's brow wrinkled as she cleared her throat. "Your father told me to give this to you for your initiation tonight. I do not know what is inside."

Juliet was so distraught she could not bear to look at the contents herself. "Open it, will you?"

The nurse lifted the lid and peered inside, then bowed her head in dismay.

"Weapons, my child. Of all sorts," the nurse mumbled.

Another surge of rage bolted through Juliet. She charged toward the nurse—practically knocking the woman over—and slammed the box shut with a ter-rifying animalistic growl that was quite similar to her father's. Then she flopped down on the gray wool rug, her breath coming in short spurts.

"They want me to kill Romeo." Juliet held back tears as the nurse sat down next to her. "Please, good Nurse, I need your counsel more than ever."

The nurse stroked Juliet's hair with her fingertips. "Try not to worry, Juliet. If Romeo has any sense, he has hidden himself far from anyone's reach. Even you would be unable to find him."

"But that's not the point," Juliet said, pushing the nurse's hand away. "Regardless of who I take as my first kill tonight, tomorrow my parents will force me to marry Count Paris. There is just no end to their cruelty."

"Madam, I think your passion is clouding your judgment," the nurse said, her voice calm and soothing. "If you look at this situation with a clear mind and an unaffected heart, you'll see that Romeo has nothing to offer you, especially now that he is exiled. Count Paris is not perfect, but he can provide for you and help your parents protect your family. Please, take his hand, child. Spare yourself any more torment and choose security in the long run over happiness in the now."

"Do you speak from your heart?" Juliet whimpered.

"And my soul, too. Or else curse them both."

Juliet turned and looked directly at the nurse. She realized, then and there, that she could no longer go to this woman for help or even sympathy. Though still caring and nurturing, the nurse was on the side of

Lord and Lady Capulet, and nothing could be done about it. That meant there was only one person left who Juliet could trust. She must go to him—now—and see if he could assist her. If not, then she would have to face her fate alone.

"Well, then, you have convinced me," Juliet said with a suddenly amiable spirit.

The nurse seemed quite baffled. "What?"

"I have found such comfort in your wisdom, friend," Juliet explained as she slid the metal box out from under her bed. "I will venture into the forest and practice my hunting skills. Would you go into town and buy the finest wedding dresses you can find? I'll want to choose one later."

"Yes, of course." The nurse cracked a smile. "I am most happy to."

"Speak nothing of it, though. I want my mother to be surprised when I tell her I've reconsidered," she added.

As soon as the nurse left the room, Juliet reopened the box and marveled at the killing tools inside. She ran her thumb along the blade of a short sword, hoping she would have the will to use it on herself if her last grasp at good fortune failed her.

CHAPTER SIXTEEN

ater that evening, Juliet was at the front door of the monastery once again, hunched over in more pain. She had recalled how anxious she had been right before her marriage to Romeo, but the dread and suffering she felt right at this moment was infinitely worse. With one hand on her belly, she knocked at the door. Moments later, it opened a crack, and she saw the friendly eyes of Friar Laurence, peeking out from behind it.

He recognized Juliet at once and welcomed her into the monastery, leading her to his private cell. Juliet bowed her head as she floated down the hallway.

"Friar, I am desperate for your help," she said.

"Of course, child. What can I do for you?" the friar asked, placing a warm hand on her pale cheek.

"That is the trouble. I am not a child anymore,"

Juliet said, lifting her gaze toward him. "Yesterday, I became Romeo's wife, and today, I am a vampire. In the next few hours, my life will be beyond repair."

"Do not lose hope just yet. I might be able to help you."

Juliet floated away from the friar and toward an oval-shaped stained-glass window. She peered through the tinted glass at purple trees and a yellow sky.

"You know that the Capulets are born human and transition into vampires on the day they turn sixteen."

"Yes, that is common knowledge to practically everyone in Transylvania," Friar Laurence replied.

"Well, no one outside of the vampire world is aware of the initiation rite that must be performed by midnight of every Capulet's sixteenth birthday," Juliet went on.

"You are right, I don't know what you are talking about," the friar said.

"What I am going to tell you must remain a secret. Promise me you will not repeat any of this to a living soul," Juliet demanded.

"I promise."

Juliet traced the outline of Romeo's name on the window with her pointy fingernails. "In order to achieve immortality and full admission into the vampire race, one must leave the castle alone and hunt down a human."

She put a hand on her chest in an attempt to quiet her racing heart.

"Then what?" Friar Laurence asked.

"He or she must kill the person and drink the victim's blood," Juliet said.

The friar barely reacted. "You are a vampire, Juliet, and a Capulet, so this news is hardly surprising."

"True, but this goes against every principle and value that I hold dear, and if I do not perform this act today, I will be *dead* by morning," she said, her voice cracking. "Before I met Romeo, I was willing to sacrifice my life for what I believed in. But now I cherish every waking moment I share with him and cannot even begin to think of leaving him behind—in life or death."

The friar remained silent, clearly contemplating what Juliet had just confided in him.

"Within me, there is a raging hunger for human blood that the normal girl I was before had promised herself she would never submit to. Lord and Lady Capulet are forcing me to use Romeo as my initiation kill and avenge my cousin Tybalt's death. They are also making me marry another vampire tomorrow. How can I even think of betraying my love like that?" Juliet broke into tears, pounding her fist on the window in agony. "This is why I came to see you."

Without hesitating, the friar approached her and took hold of her hand. "Your story is most woeful, my lady. No one would deny that. What does Romeo think you should do?"

A tear dribbled down the side of Juliet's somber face. "He does not know about the initiation rite, or my arranged engagement to Count Paris."

The friar sighed and gave a disapproving look.

"I tried to tell him this morning, Friar, but we ran out of time," Juliet explained. "And now I have no idea where he is, so I cannot possibly tell him."

Friar Laurence took her hand in his. "If you had made your confession to him, I am sure he would understand, being that he, too, has been forced to take a life."

"It is not the same thing. He and his friend were being attacked." Juliet pulled away gently. "I would have to hurt someone who has done nothing against me. Or as my family sees it, strike down the only man I will ever love."

"Well, my lady, I have been worried about your future with Romeo since I married you two," the friar said. "Not that I doubt your feelings for each other, but because you come from such different worlds, you were bound to run into trouble. I believe I have found a solution, though."

Juliet's eyes widened with surprise. "You have?"

"Please, come with me to the library. I will explain everything there."

Juliet felt another brutal twinge inside her stomach, causing her to lurch forward. She was willing to do anything to free herself from these chains. "Yes, of course."

The library was on the top floor of the monastery, a large, airy room with two windows on either side. A painting of the Last Supper was hung on the left wall. On the right were numerous shelves, cabinets, and such, stacked with volumes of books.

The friar wandered over to a waist-high bookcase. He crouched down and ran his finger along the leather spines, looking carefully at each title until he found one with gold-stitched lettering: *The Revival of Virtue*. He pulled the book from the top shelf and flipped through it, whipping through the yellowed pages with great speed.

All of a sudden the friar stopped and pointed to a lengthy paragraph in the center column. "Here, Juliet. Look at this."

Friar Laurence handed Juliet the bulky volume, which somehow felt light as a feather in her grasp. She set her flaming red eyes on the paragraph and read:

For centuries, many theologians have believed that the road to salvation for the undead rests in scripture, especially Matthew 5:13–16.

"You are the salt of the earth; but if salt has lost its taste, how can its flavor be restored?"

Based on this passage, missionaries have made numerous attempts to help members of the Underworld become human again by drinking blood from a vampire corpse, which has been purified with salt. Most of these trials failed, but there is rumored to be one successful case—when the body had gone through rigor mortis (roughly thirty-six hours after death) and the blood was purified using a combination of three salts of the earth—pink, black, and sea. After this blood was properly cleansed and ingested by the hellion, he returned to the human state he was in prior to his vampirism.

Juliet couldn't believe what she was reading. There was a way for her to remain human, just like her husband! She was so excited by this new hope that her lips turned up into a wide smile. But when she came to the end of the paragraph, her eyes became misty with tears.

However, this process is rarely carried out because of the difficulty of procuring the three different salts, which originate from remote areas of the world.

Juliet slammed the book shut, her bottom lip trembling. "Is this some kind of cruel trick?"

The friar's brow wrinkled with confusion. "What? I'm only trying to help you."

"But it's written here in plain English—the salts that are needed for the purification process are scattered all around the globe," Juliet said, sniffling. "It will be too difficult to attempt it."

"Difficult but not impossible." Friar Laurence rubbed his hands together and smiled. "I know a shaman who lives in seclusion in Moldova. He might have all of the salts."

Juliet raised her eyebrows. "Really?"

"Yes," the friar reassured her. "But to be honest, the more difficult task will be finding a vampire corpse. Unless . . ."

"What, Friar? Tell me," Juliet said.

Friar Laurence took a deep breath and finished his thought. "Unless I ask the Montagues for Tybalt's body."

Juliet felt a faint spell coming over her, but fortunately, she was able to resist it. The thought of drinking Tybalt's blood made her feel guilty and nauseated. Yet it was the only way that she could turn back the hands of time and give her and Romeo a real chance. Perhaps then Tybalt's death would not totally be in vain.

"Let it be done, Friar, and quickly," Juliet said, clutching at her stomach, which growled again with insatiable hunger. "I want nothing more than to live a normal, human life with my dear Romeo."

"I want that for you, too. But first we have to make sure that time stands still," the friar added as he walked over to a mahogany desk. "I need at least a day to get the salts and the body, and we must halt the progression of your condition so you will live past midnight and beyond, without ever having to kill."

The friar pulled a skeleton key out of his robe pocket and held it up in the air for a brief inspection. Then he inserted it into one of the desk drawers, unlocking it with a loud click.

"Besides, it seems clear that the Capulets' and Montagues' hatred for each other will never cease. They might do anything to keep you and Romeo apart. The only way to ensure they will not interfere is for you to convince them you are no longer alive."

Juliet looked on with awe as Friar Laurence placed a small lead box on top of the desk. He opened the box carefully and took out a tiny glass vial filled with a blue liquid.

"This potion will put you into a trancelike state and slow down all your bodily functions for twenty-four hours. You will be able to hear and see, but you will not be able to move or speak. And to everyone, you will appear to be truly dead—not undead," the friar explained. "By the time the potion wears off, you will most likely be lying inside your family's crypt. Your parents will have held a funeral for you and buried you there."

"What then, Friar? How will Romeo know what has happened?" Juliet said, jumping to the final piece of the puzzle.

"I must admit, I know Romeo's whereabouts."

Juliet blinked in disbelief. "You do?"

"Yes, but I was told not to share it with anyone, including you. For your own protection, of course," the friar said.

Although Juliet was desperate to know where her husband was, she nodded in affirmation. After all that he had done for her and Romeo, she trusted the friar completely.

"Drink this no less than an hour before midnight." Friar Laurence put the vial in Juliet's quaking hand. "I will send two of my friars as messengers. One to go to the shaman and the other to Romeo to alert him of the plan. Romeo will come to rescue you from the crypt and bring you back to my cell for the purification ceremony. Then you both will be free to go anywhere in the world to live in peace."

"Thank you, dear Friar," Juliet said, and kissed the man on the cheek. "If I survive this, I will make sure we name our firstborn son after you."

The friar's cheeks flushed a shade of red similar to Juliet's glowing eyes. "What an honor that would be."

CHAPTER SEVENTEEN

Just outside the Moldovan border, Romeo cowered in the corner of a dilapidated wooden shack, blowing onto his hands in order to keep them warm. Once the sun had set a couple of hours ago, the temperature had dropped substantially, forcing him to battle the evening chill. As the sky continued to darken, he reminded himself that this abandoned shanty was only a temporary lodging, until Friar Laurence could find someone to provide him with what he hoped would be a less dilapidated sanctuary. Hopefully in a day or two, he would be settled and rested enough to return to Transylvania, like he'd promised Juliet.

That is, if he didn't freeze to death first.

Romeo pulled his knees up to his chest, his teeth chattering as a burst of howling wind whizzed through the holes in the roof. To distract himself, he closed his eyes and tried to picture what Juliet was doing at that moment. Surprisingly, all that this did was to make him even more upset. Although he had just shared the most spectacular night of his life with Juliet, ever since he crawled out of her window, Romeo could not stop worrying about the initiation rite that Juliet never fully explained. It had his wife so upset, she could barely even speak of it.

And midnight would soon be upon them.

Outside the shack, there were noises—the sound of snapping twigs and tree branches being chopped by a machete. Immediately, Romeo sprang into action, his frigid hands grabbing a parrying dagger from his bootstrap. Once he had it in his grip, he pulled his arm back, preparing to throw the dagger if one of Prince Radu's rogue soldiers—or worse, an enraged Capulet—stormed through the feeble entrance. The wind was now frenzied, its high-pitched shrieking piercing Romeo's ears.

This was why he did not hear anyone knocking.

Just as the door flew open, Romeo threw the dagger without even looking at the heavily cloaked intruder. The weapon sailed across the small shanty and planted itself firmly in the assailant's right arm. The man screamed out angrily and dropped to his knees.

"Damn you, Romeo!"

There was no mistaking the voice.

"Benvolio?" Romeo said.

The man pulled back the hood on his black cloak and revealed his face.

Romeo knelt down next to Benvolio, hanging his head in shame. "Have mercy on me, Cousin. I had no idea it was you."

"I am not so sure," Benvolio said, wincing in pain.

Romeo reached out to inspect Benvolio's arm, but his cousin yanked it away. "Let me have a look at your wound."

"Have you become a doctor in the hours you've been out here?" Benvolio said sarcastically.

"No, but I have mastered the art of street fighting, so I would watch my step if I were you." Romeo snagged Benvolio by the elbow and yanked his arm toward the bit of moonlight that was peeking through the cracks in the wall planks.

"All of Transylvania knows that now," Benvolio said, a small hint of pride tingeing his usually brutish tone.

Romeo ignored these words and peered at his cousin's injured biceps. "Luckily, the blade did not go too far beneath the skin."

"Well, it seems as though the master street fighter still has more to learn when it comes to his aim and technique," Benvolio said.

"Hold still while I take this out." Romeo took the handle of the dagger in his right hand, gripping it tightly.

Benvolio gritted his teeth and clenched both his fists. "Fine, just hurry up."

Romeo breathed in deeply and pulled the dagger out of Benvolio's arm in one fast, easy motion. Benvolio grunted loudly and covered the open, bloody wound with his hand.

"Wait, we have to wrap that cut in something," Romeo said with concern.

"I dare you to find something clean in here, Dr. Montague," Benvolio retorted.

Romeo reached into his jacket pocket and grasped a bottle of holy water, which Friar Laurence had given him as a small measure of protection before he left Transylvania. He tore off a piece of fabric from the bottom of his shirt and doused it with the water. Then he placed the soaked shred of garment on Benvolio's upper arm, tying it off in a knot.

"There, that ought to do it," he said.

Benvolio snarled unhappily. "I guess you're quite pleased with yourself now, aren't you?"

Romeo just smirked and said nothing.

"Well I wouldn't have needed this tourniquet if it wasn't for your stupidity," Benvolio chided him.

"Why the hell are you here anyway, Benvolio?" Romeo said with a resigned sigh.

Benvolio got up off the ground and went outside, returning with a large sack, much like the one

Mercutio had brought to Capulet Castle a few days prior. Romeo's heart ached at the thought of his friend and the look on his face when he died.

Benvolio threw the sack on the floor. "I brought you some provisions. Blankets, clothes, food, more weapons, and more holy water, just in case any of the Capulets manage to find you. All of the townspeople contributed these goods, and one of the friars at the monastery told me where I could deliver them."

A sizable lump formed in Romeo's throat. "I do not deserve their charity."

"Why not? You avenged Mercutio's death and slew Tybalt Capulet like a true Montague. Don't you under-stand? You are a hero in everyone's eyes," Benvolio said while mussing up Romeo's hair.

Romeo swatted Benvolio's hand away, then rose to his feet and confronted his cousin. "Everyone's but my own."

"Are you saying you have no right to be proud of what you have done?" Benvolio asked incredulously.

"What I have done? I killed a man, Benvolio. How do you expect me to celebrate that?"

Benvolio got within one inch of Romeo's face, his rough skin turning bright pink. "You killed a *monster*, Romeo. A hideous, disgusting monster that attacked and killed your closest friend! Why on God's earth would you feel any remorse?"

"It isn't that simple!" Romeo barked.

Benvolio laughed in annoyance. "I cannot think of anything simpler than standing up for your kinsmen and friends. That is what brought me here."

Romeo felt a sharp twinge in his gut. Was he disrespecting his cousin and the memory of Mercutio by feeling guilty about taking Tybalt's life? The ever-loyal Benvolio certainly seemed to believe so.

But there was so much that Benvolio didn't know. And there was no way Romeo could tell him, or any other Montague, that he had chosen a Capulet—a vampire—as his wife. It would lead to total anarchy, and God only knew how many more people would die.

"Thank you, Benvolio. I appreciate your help, I really do," Romeo said, his voice soft and humble.

Benvolio rubbed his arm and smirked. "You certainly have a peculiar way of showing it."

Romeo could not help but chuckle, even though another bone-chilling gust whipped through the walls of the shack.

"Do my mother and father know about this?" Romeo had a strong feeling that he already knew the answer to this question, but he prayed that Benvolio's reply would prove him wrong.

"Yes, we were able to get word to them in Serbia," Benvolio replied.

Romeo ran his hands through his hair and sighed. "What do you think will happen once they return to Transylvania?"

"Well, they will most likely round up the troops and carry out another raid on the Capulets, to avenge you and Mercutio," said Benvolio.

Apparently, the violence that Romeo had feared would erupt if his family found out about him and Juliet was going to occur anyway.

"We cannot let them do that!" he exclaimed, hitting the wall hard with his fist.

"Why not? None of us truly believed that Radu's treaty would be able to control the vicious acts of the Capulets. They are beasts, can't you see that?"

"But when will it stop, Benvolio? How much killing will it take to make either side see that fighting isn't going to solve anything?" Romeo shouted.

"The killing will stop once vampires like the Capulets are wiped off the face of the earth!" Benvolio roared. "I believe that now more than ever."

Romeo threw his arms up in defeat. "It is impossible to talk to you, Benvolio. You are so filled with anger and hate that you cannot even think straight."

"When it comes to the Capulets, yes, I am," Benvolio admitted. "But I do not feel any shame over that. Mercy is for *people*, Romeo—people who care for their fellow man. Innocent people who just want to live a simple life. Mercy is not for the enemy."

Romeo shook his head. He hated to give up on his cousin—and his entire family—but it didn't look like he had another choice. The Montagues seemed to want the violence to continue, just as much as the Capulets did. All the more reason for him and Juliet to get out of Transylvania and find a place where they could love each other forever.

"Then I guess there is nothing more for us to say on the matter, is there?"

Benvolio defiantly crossed his arms in front of his chest. "No, there isn't."

Romeo was quiet for a moment before engaging his cousin again. "Did the friar happen to tell you how much longer I would have to stay here?"

"I do not know, although I gather it will be for quite some time," Benvolio stated.

"Why do you say that?" Romeo rubbed his hands together to prevent them from going numb from the cold.

"A two-week quarantine was just issued in this region," Benvolio explained. "Smallpox is tearing through here like a storm. Absolutely no one is allowed to travel outside of their homes or cross the border. So consider yourself trapped in isolation for a while."

Romeo's eyes opened wide with alarm. Two weeks before he could get to Juliet? That was absolutely out of the question. If he waited that long, she would certainly think he had deserted her. There was no way he could send Benvolio back with a message either, or anyone else, for that matter. Romeo had no other choice.

"I must go back with you, Benvolio!" he said urgently.

"Are you insane? I barely made it here myself without getting caught by both the Wallachian and Moldovan militias," Benvolio replied. "You have to stay here."

"But I need—" Romeo tried to protest, but Benvolio grabbed him by the shoulders and shook him hard.

"Whatever it is that you need in Transylvania is not worth dying for," his cousin said sternly.

And yet it was. A million times over.

CHAPTER EIGHTEEN

The Great Hall was buzzing with prewedding activity when Juliet had returned to the castle at a quarter to ten. As she floated above the freshly mopped floor, she dodged a group of servants who were rearranging all of the furniture in the room to make way for the Capulets' guests. Large bouquets of red chrysanthemums and yellow lilies were scattered about in crystal vases. Clearly, the Capulets were sparing no expense for the wedding of their only child. Perhaps under other circumstances, Juliet would have been flattered by all of this fuss.

Lady Capulet stood at the top of the staircase, keeping a close eye on the hired help as they wrapped swaths of purple-stained fabric around marble columns.

"Stop, stop. It's supposed to look elegant, not gaudy!" she shouted.

Juliet ran her fingertips along the wooden banister as she ascended the stairs, rehearsing in her mind the simple script she and the friar had created right before she left the monastery. She hoped that she would be able to convince Lady Capulet that she'd had a change of heart—her future with Romeo depended on that.

Then again, Juliet could not help but feel somewhat selfish for playing this cruel trick on her mother, who was looking just as ill as she had looked this morning. Was it fair for her to choose her life with Romeo over the lives of all the Capulets? If someone had asked Juliet this question an hour ago at the monastery, she would have said yes, but now that she was standing in the commanding presence of her own mother, she was not sure what her answer would be.

Juliet smoothed out her dress and approached Lady Capulet. "Good evening, Mother."

While Lady Capulet acknowledged Juliet's presence with a quick nod of her head, she kept her fierce red eyes trained on the commotion in the Great Hall.

"I want to apologize for how I behaved earlier," Juliet went on, trying the best she could to gain her mother's forgiveness. "I was incredibly rude, and you deserve so much more respect than that. You and Father have given me everything I could ever want. I should never have turned my back on you."

Her mother put her hands on her small waist and turned toward Juliet. "So have you truly come to your senses? Or should I expect another tantrum by the time this conversation is through?"

Juliet felt every muscle in her body tense up, but when she put her hand in her skirt pocket and felt the vial of potion in her hand, she was able to contain her emotions.

"I'm sorry, my lady," Juliet said most humbly. "I finally see how wrong I have been and I do not wish to anger or disappoint you and Father any more than I already have."

Lady Capulet stood still, the stern look on her slowly eroding face receded.

"Being a Capulet and protecting our heritage is important to me, honestly." Juliet was practically choking on these false words. Each time she apologized for doing what she knew in her heart was right, or lied about her emotions, she could feel a fierce wave of heat sting her skin from head to toe. But she managed to soldier on by reminding herself that at this time tomorrow, she would be human again and in Romeo's arms.

"So tonight, I will perform the initiation, and tomorrow I will marry Count Paris," Juliet proclaimed.

"I am happy you have seen the light." Lady Capulet took Juliet's free hand and squeezed it softly in her own.

"I am, too, Mother," Juliet said, lowering her eyes.

"You have the weapons from your father. Now hurry along. You only have an hour for hunting," Lady

Capulet added matter-of-factly. "Our guards have some suggestions on where to find Romeo Montague, so you should consult with them before you depart. But that is all the help you are allowed. The initiation rite is about embracing your destiny, and you must do it alone."

"I understand," Juliet said with a lump the size of a stone lodged in her throat.

"It is customary that we do not see each other again until you are a full-fledged vampire so I will come to your chambers at dusk," Lady Capulet instructed. "Now go. Your nurse is waiting in your chambers."

"Thank you," Juliet replied, curtsying.

"Good luck," her mother said, her watchful gaze returning to the wedding decorations.

Juliet nodded and smiled, then turned around and floated down the corridor to her chambers. Once she flung open the door, she saw her nurse laying out two garments upon her bed—an off-the-shoulder white silk dupioni gown with double lantern sleeves and shimmering gold fabric along the neckline, and an ivory satin floor-length dress with a silk brocade bodice and several layers of deep pleating in the skirt. Both of them were far superior to the simple housedress she had worn to her wedding with Romeo, and yet to Juliet's eyes neither of them was as beautiful.

"Welcome home, my lady," the nurse said without so much as a glance in Juliet's direction. The oil lamp on the nightstand flickered and cast an eerie shadow on the wall behind her.

"Thank you, Nurse." Juliet remained in the doorway. A voice in her head was begging her to run from this awkward scene, but she forbade herself from listening to it.

"I hope all went well in the forest earlier." The nurse took three steps back from Juliet's bed, and then turned to face the girl she had helped raise. "Is everything as it should be, child?"

Juliet glided toward the nurse, her hands folded in front of her. "I suppose it is. I just told Lady Capulet I will go through with both the initiation and the wedding."

The nurse approached Juliet and held her arms out for a hug, which Juliet did not refuse. "I am so delighted for you, madam."

Juliet was so anxious, she was surprised she could even breathe. Although she believed in what she was doing, she hadn't realized how difficult it would be to lie to the people who were closest to her. After Friar Laurence's plan had succeeded, would Juliet be able to live with the guilt?

When a vivid picture of Romeo's face flashed in her mind, she instantly knew the answer to that question.

Yes.

Juliet wiggled out of the nurse's tight hold and moved toward the window, turning her back to the nurse. "Now leave me be, will you?"

"But what about your wedding dress?"

Juliet peered over her shoulder and gave the woman a loving look—one that was not fake in the least. She and the nurse did not see eye to eye, but the woman cared for her more than anyone else in the world.

Except for Juliet's husband, of course.

"I won't be able to marry Count Paris tomorrow evening if I do not make my first kill in an hour. Please let me go."

"As you wish." The nurse picked up a small sewing kit off the ground and smiled. "We'll decide on the dress tomorrow, once you wake up."

"Thank you."

With that, the nurse scurried out of Juliet's chambers and closed the door behind her.

Stabbing sensations pierced Juliet's side as she raced to the door and shoved a high-backed chair underneath the knob so that it could not be opened from the outside. Then she looked at the white gowns that were placed on her bedspread so neatly by her nurse. Juliet did think the silk one was stunning and exactly the kind of dress she would have picked out for herself. Her heart fluttered when she thought what Romeo might think if he saw her in it.

Juliet held the dress up to her chest and reached for the hand mirror that was on top of her vanity. But when she placed the looking glass in front of her face, there was no reflection to greet her—just the gold neckline of the gown, hovering in the dim light like a ghost.

Juliet was so horrified that she dropped the mirror on the floor, shattering the glass into jagged little pieces. She stumbled back toward the bed, clutching the dress to her chest. Her head hung low and tears stung her red eyes. The realization that she would never see her reflection again had shaken her to her very core, but when she lifted her head up and noticed that her body no longer cast a shadow, she angrily threw both gowns at the wall and screamed.

Juliet covered her face with her hands, her cheeks feeling hot to the touch. She took a few deep breaths, slowly transforming her anguish into resolve and purpose. She reminded herself that her descent into vampirism—and madness—would end the moment she and Romeo reunited with the friar at the monastery, so she should not delay the plan any longer. After a few cleansing breaths, she dug into her skirt pocket once more and grabbed the vial filled with Friar Laurence's potion, imagining what the future with Romeo would look like, with herself fully human again.

Without a single shred of fear in her heart or mind, she held up the vial and said, "Romeo, I come! This do I drink to thee!" Then she drank the contents, gulping the liquid down until none was left. There was no wait for the concoction to take effect. Instantly, Juliet's legs gave out, causing her to fall on the mattress, her arms trapped beneath her weight and her head turned to the side.

Soon, Juliet's entire body was completely numb. Just as the friar warned, she could not move any of her limbs, nor could she speak a word. But she could hear the sound of the wind banging against the window shutters, and watch the flame of the oil lamp dance like a drunken Gypsy, and count the minutes until she could kiss Romeo's sweet lips over and over and over again.

As nightfall descended upon Transylvania the following day, the nurse discovered Juliet, sprawled out on her bed with her eyes wide open and her body as limp as the stem of a dying flower. It was almost eighteen hours since Juliet had drunk Friar Laurence's potion— and the nurse had just broken down the door with a battle-ax after she could not gain entrance to the room and Juliet did not respond to her calls.

"Dear God! No! NO!" the nurse cried out as she collapsed onto the floor, clutching at Juliet's lifeless legs. "Oh, what terrible thing have you done to yourself, child?!"

Juliet stared out into space and listened as the nurse sobbed uncontrollably. With each gasp for air, the woman kept shouting the word "no," as if protesting would make Juliet come alive again.

"Please, merciful Lord," the nurse said through a

cascade of tears. "Welcome this wonderful, darling creature into your kingdom. I raised and loved her as if she were my own. How I will miss her!"

As she witnessed her nurse unravel at the sight of her seemingly dead body, a hundred memories of the tender moments they had shared flashed through Juliet's mind—their summertime walks across the castle's great lawn; the delicious custard tarts they used to make from scratch; the leather-bound books they read by the fire. She was so touched by the nurse's intense and all-encompassing grief that she wanted to break through her trance and hug the woman who had made such a long-lasting impression on her.

But it would be several more hours before Juliet could move a finger.

Her hearing, though, was still acute. While the nurse continued to cry, Juliet could make out some sounds coming from the hallway—doors creaking open and the hum of soft, sleepy voices. Soon Lady Capulet entered the room with great alarm. Clearly, she had been awakened by the nurse's loud wailing. She glided over to the other side of the bed, knelt down, and placed a hand on the crown of her daughter's head.

"What happened, Nurse? Did Juliet return from her hunt very sick?" Lady Capulet asked as she stroked Juliet's hair with her quaking fingers.

"My lady, she is gone," the nurse said, sniffling.

"She is gone from us forever!"

Juliet watched as her mother looked deep into her eyes for any sign of life. When she could find none, Lady Capulet brought her quivering hand up to her mouth. Then she buried her face in her daughter's soft brown locks.

"My sweet, beautiful, precious child!" Lady Capulet's moans of anguish were muffled by the mattress upon which Juliet lay still. "This cannot be real. You cannot be dead. I won't believe it!"

Juliet felt a jolt of fear tweak her brain. Could her mother actually sense the truth—that her daughter's body would awaken from this drug-induced state and eventually live as a human, just as she had days before?

Then again, Juliet had all night and day to wonder what her mother's reaction would be, and none of the scenes she pictured involved Lady Capulet shedding one tear. But here she was, being cradled and mourned by her mother, the sternest vampire she'd ever known.

As Juliet gazed into her mother's face, she felt a twinge of pity. With fresh new cracks in her skin, Lady Capulet was growing weaker. Who knew how long it would be before her mother lost a good portion of her supernatural powers. Then again, Juliet was hopeful that in the wake of her death, Lady Capulet would realize that there were more important things in life than superhuman strength and wealth and prestige and vampire supremacy.

The nurse got up from the floor and shuffled over to Lady Capulet, wiping at her eyes and nose. "It hurts me to repeat this, my lady, but it is true. Our Juliet is not of this world any longer."

Lady Capulet reeled back from the bed, but refused to let go of her daughter, clinging to one of Juliet's hands. "I never thought my heart could break like this."

Suddenly a voice boomed from behind Juliet.

"What is going on in here? I could hear all your shrieking from my chambers."

Juliet recognized the commanding speaker instantly. Her father, Lord Capulet, had finally arrived on the scene.

"The universe has smote us, Husband," Lady Capulet bellowed. "And taken our only child from us."

Out of the corner of her eye, Juliet saw her father come close to the bed and glower down at her with a blank expression frozen on his face. His tough facade did not crack like Lady Capulet's had—not in the slightest.

"No, my lady. Juliet has taken her own life," Lord Capulet scolded. "She stood by her threats and refused to go through with the initiation. In doing so, she denied her destiny. Death is just in this matter."

"It is not respectful to speak ill of the dead, my lord," the nurse blurted out, then bowed her head in submission as Lord Capulet bared his sharp fangs and growled.

"We never should have foisted these burdens upon

her," murmured a distraught Lady Capulet. "She was too young, and too frightened."

"She was disloyal!" Juliet heard her father shout. "She knew that we needed her to coax Count Paris into an alliance with us. Now we might lose every treasure we have fought for."

Juliet observed her mother's piercing gaze as she got up to combat Lord Capulet. It was the first time in all her life that she was not scared of that fierce look.

"We should have helped her!" Lady Capulet snapped. "Instead, we ignored all of her pleas for understanding. When she begged us not to force her into marriage, we were self-righteous and unrelenting. When she told us she could not go through with her first kill, we were dismissive and unkind. Now look where that has gotten all of us?"

"There was nothing we could have done about the count. We had to think of our people first!" Lord Capulet yelled. "And there was no way to avoid the initiation. Every vampire must undergo it!"

"What about the purification ritual?" Lady Capulet said, shoving her husband's shoulders with both her hands.

"I told you, that is a ludicrous myth," her father replied angrily.

Her mother looked up to the sky, choking back more tears. "Even so, we could have tried it. But we were so concerned with keeping our power."

Juliet felt as though someone had thrown her body into a fire pit. If both her parents had known all along that there might be a chance—however slim it was—to spare Juliet this cruel fate, and plainly ignored it, how could she ever forgive them?

"And what is wrong with that?" Lord Capulet argued. "Without the use of our powers, we cannot fight off the humans or sufficiently protect one single thing that we have. If everything we've acquired is taken from us, we will live forever with that thorn in our pride. And when that happens, the vampire race can blame our daughter and this stunt of hers."

"Stunt?!" Lady Capulet struck her husband hard across the face. "She is dead!"

Lord Capulet remained unmoved.

"I suppose you better start planning her funeral service while I try to appease Count Paris," he said coldly.

Then he exited Juliet's chambers, without shedding a single tear for her.

CHAPTER NINETEEN

 s Romeo crawled through the mud in a vast field, just outside the Moldovan border, he prayed that the country's patrolling soldiers, who were less than five hundred yards away, would not notice him making his escape. He slithered through the rain-soaked blades of grass like a snake, keeping his head down low. All he had to do to slip back into Transylvania was cross this pasture and find the small, rugged, and rarely traveled path that he'd taken to Moldova only a day ago. The dirt road would lead through the valleys of the Carpathian Mountains and, eventually, back to his home village—and his dearest, most precious love.

Romeo's arms and legs ached from pushing through the soft, wet dirt, his fingers tired of dragging a burlap sack alongside him. But once he saw the end of the field and a collection of tall spruce trees that surrounded the opening of the path, his body felt as fresh as morning dew. As soon as he reached the patch of trees, Romeo quickly ducked behind one and untied the top of the sack. He took off his soiled shirt and pants and put on the new clothes that Benvolio had brought for him. They were a tad baggy on Romeo's lean frame, but that did not matter. He planned on wearing a long, hooded black cloak, which would hide his highly recognizable face and figure when he arrived in Transylvania.

Before putting on the cloak, Romeo took an oblong glass vial filled with holy water and shoved it into his right trouser pocket. In an angry Capulet mob-related emergency, Romeo would only need a few drops of it to burn their skin and send them running in the other direction. But that was a confrontation he hoped would never happen. There had been enough violence over the past couple of days.

By around nine o'clock that evening, he arrived in Transylvania and went directly to a small neighbor-hood pub in the center of town. He found a good table in the corner, where he could be alone, and sat down. The hood of his dark cloak hung loosely over his fore-head. So far, neither the townspeople nor the prince's cavalry had recognized him, which was certainly a blessing.

As Romeo sipped on a mug of freshly decanted ale, his eyes scanned the crowd for Juliet's nurse or Maribel, the servant maid who had helped him,

Benvolio, and Mercutio gain access to Capulet Castle on the night of the ball. Romeo knew this pub was usually frequented by the servants at the castle, and he was hoping that at some point, either Maribel or the nurse would come walking through the doors. All he needed was two minutes alone with one of them in order to relay a message to Juliet.

What that message would be, Romeo was still unsure. He and Juliet had promised each other that they would leave Transylvania together and never look back—but what of Juliet's initiation rite, this act she had been so terrified of committing? Romeo knew that whatever she'd done, he loved her enough to look past it.

Didn't he?

Romeo took another swig of ale and swallowed hard. He kept his gaze locked on the entrance to the pub and tried to block out negative thoughts. But when the front door creaked open and two of Prince Radu's soldiers sauntered in, carrying their shields under their arms, his entire body went ice cold. He lowered his head, ducking his chin to his chest, as the two men sat at a table no more than a few feet away from him. The pudgier soldier raised his hand, signaling the barkeep, while the slimmer one glanced around.

"Still looking for Romeo Montague, are you?" the heavy one asked with a hearty chuckle.

"I suppose I shouldn't be, but I have this odd feeling that he is right under our noses," the thin one replied.

Romeo nearly spit out his ale.

"The whole cavalry is still on high alert," said the thin soldier. "He never would come back and risk his neck."

"It's too bad. The boy is going to miss out on the big celebration," the heavy one replied.

The thin solider seemed annoyed. "I wasn't notified of any celebration."

"I'm assuming there will be one, once word travels from Capulet Castle to the Montague homestead."

The barkeep appeared and placed two small shots of liquor in front of the soldiers. Romeo took this opportunity to move over to the far end of the bench he was sitting on so he could listen more intently to the men. It seemed as though their conversation was about to become very interesting. He did not want to miss a minute of it—perhaps they had information that might help him set up a rendezvous with Juliet.

"What happened at the castle?" the thin soldier said as he drank.

"I had to transport Count Paris there just before sunset—in a horse-drawn carriage and coffin no less!" the heavy soldier said, shuddering at the thought of it. "Apparently, that is how he must travel when the sun is out."

The thin soldier guffawed. "That is quite possibly the most absurd thing I have ever heard."

"Hold on to your bootstraps. There is more," the heavy soldier teased.

Romeo leaned in a little farther, trying not to be too conspicuous. He had never heard of this Count Paris before, but it sounded as though he was a vampire of great importance, if the prince's men were involved with him.

"Apparently, the count was set to marry Lord Capulet's daughter tonight," the heavy soldier went on. "In a grandiose ceremony, fit for the highest ranks of royalty."

All of a sudden Romeo's head felt as though someone were pounding on it with the end of a quarterstaff. There had to be some mistake. Juliet was already his wife! How could she possibly be marrying another? Then again, what if this was the initiation rite she was condemned to perform? That could explain how reluctant and afraid she was to tell him about it. Romeo rubbed at his temples and tried to compose himself.

"However, the bride never made it to the altar," the soldier added.

Romeo put a hand on his chest and let out a cleansing sigh of relief.

"Was it a case of wedding-day jitters?" the thin soldier asked. "Or did she run into the arms of another one of her kind?"

"Neither," the heavy one answered. "She was found dead in her chambers by her nurse—from suicide, the guards said. They just held her funeral and soon she will be laid in a tomb within the Capulet family crypt."

Romeo swore that he felt the blood in his veins turn to fire and his flesh burn right off of his bones.

"I hope Count Paris does not take it personally," the thin one said, laughing.

Romeo's ears were ringing so loudly he could not hear the two soldiers talk anymore. His eyesight was so blurred with tears that he could barely stagger over to the front door. Why would Juliet do this to herself, when they both had so much to live for? Romeo could not make any sense of it, and now that his love was dead, he never would be able to.

Once he exited the pub, Romeo lunged at the first person he saw on the street—a blond-haired boy around the same age as he.

"Do you know where I can find an apothecary?" he said, his voice rife with agony. If he could not share his life with Juliet on earth, then he would find another way to be with her.

"On the far north end of the forest, opposite the monastery," the boy answered.

Romeo bowed his head in thanks.

"I heard his stock is limited, sir, since the change in our regime," the boy added politely.

Romeo looked up and watched two birds, whistling and frolicking together in the clear blue sky.

"A spot of poison is all I need."

Romeo arrived at the Transylvania cemetery shortly after visiting the apothecary on the north end of the forest. When he finally came upon the Capulet crypt— an ornate structure made of stone and brick, with two large steeples and painted icons of vampires hovering over the front door—his hand instinctively went for the vial of poison stored inside his left trouser pocket.

Although he was grieving over the death of Juliet, Romeo also felt strangely exhilarated as he rolled the smooth glass container between his fingers. He knew ingesting the contents would at first render him unconscious and then slow down his heart until it stopped beating. But once he was rid of his physical self, his spiritual self would be free to go in search of the soul of his fairest love, to the ends of eternity and back again.

But before he could do that, Romeo wanted to reunite with Juliet's body and say good-bye. With his eyes stinging and his throat sore, he placed a hand on the brass door handle of the crypt and pulled it open. Behind the door lurked an ugly demon, hovering in the air with his arms crossed in front of his chest. Romeo stared into his eyes, which were the color of blood, and carefully backed away from him.

"Only family is allowed in here," the vampire said, floating toward Romeo with great speed.

Without thinking, Romeo said, "I am family."

"You hardly look like it," the vampire said as he circled around Romeo like a bird of prey. "What is your name?"

"Romeo," he answered.

"Ah, Romeo Montague, I have heard a lot about you," the vampire replied. "Prince Radu will be very unhappy to learn you have totally disregarded his sentence."

"Just let me pass," Romeo barked.

"For what purpose?" the vampire prodded.

Romeo's hands balled up into fists, and he pulled back his hood. "I have come here to mourn, not to answer to you," he said.

The vampire let out a low, menacing growl. "I believe there is a mass grave for Montagues at the bottom of the castle moat. Perhaps I could show you."

"The only place you will show me to is Juliet Capulet's tomb."

"You will not get within one hundred yards of my bride-to-be," the vampire hissed. "I will make sure of that."

Suddenly Romeo's legs felt like they were made of stone. "Count Paris, I presume" was all he could bring himself to say.

"If you do not leave now, you won't live to see tomorrow," the count said. "Prince Radu is a dear friend of mine, and I'm sure he will believe me if I tell him your demise was the result of self-defense."

Romeo laughed in the count's face. Since he already planned to die, the vampire's threats were meaningless.

"I am not leaving until I see my wife," he said with a ferocious glint in his eyes.

Count Paris seemed stunned by Romeo's revelation. His red eyes widened and his brow wrinkled with confusion. Then he growled at Romeo like one of the Capulets' hungry hellhounds.

"Juliet and I were married two days ago," Romeo went on, his voice strong and, most of all, proud. "We were soul mates, do you hear me? The strength of our love can withstand anything—even death. But I doubt that is something you could ever understand."

"You expect me to believe your lies?" Count Paris sneered. "Juliet would never stoop so low as to marry a Montague."

Romeo reached into his trouser pocket and pulled out Juliet's turquoise ring. He held it out in his palm and smiled. "If I am lying, then why would I have her most precious ring?"

Without warning, Count Paris grabbed hold of Romeo by the neck and slammed him against the door of the crypt. The ring dropped on the ground and rolled away.

"This is *your* fault!" he roared. "You killed her!"

Romeo tried to breathe, but the count's grip was crushing his throat. Still, he managed to mutter, "I would never harm her."

The vampire snarled with anger and threw Romeo to the ground, where he fell flat on his back. "Don't you see? She starved to death because she would not feed on you."

Romeo lifted his head and gazed upon the count in confusion. "You are insane."

Count Paris zoomed toward Romeo and planted his boot on his neck, right underneath the chin. He applied all the weight of his body, pinning Romeo down and nearly suffocating him.

"The initiation rite—she had to kill a human by midnight and then drink all his blood, or else starve to death by the next morning," the count disclosed.

Romeo's eyes watered as the count pressed down even harder with his boot.

"Lord Capulet told me that he and Juliet's mother pressured her into avenging Tybalt's death by making you her first kill. And now it seems abundantly clear why she chose not to," Count Paris said, his voice filled with fury.

As he began to lose consciousness, Romeo had little time to digest the meaning of what he had just learned. But when it sank in that Juliet had sacrificed her own life to save his, he was able to find the power within him to escape from the vampire's death grasp. He grabbed the sole of Count Paris's boot and pushed up hard with both arms. Once he had enough room, he rolled out from underneath the count's foothold and scrambled away. Then he stood up, reached for his leg strap, and pulled out his parrying dagger. He held the handle firmly in his hands, his chest rising and falling with each quick breath.

"Our love is eternal," Romeo said, pointing the dagger straight at the count. "Which is why neither you, nor anyone else, will prevent me from being with her."

Count Paris snickered. "Tybalt was just an overgrown child. My powers and strength are far superior than his ever were."

"Prove it, then," Romeo said through gritted teeth.

Instantly, the count lunged at Romeo, tackling him at his torso and pushing him into the black wrought-iron gate that surrounded the crypt. Romeo almost let his dagger slip out of his fingers, but thankfully he held on. Still, Count Paris had managed to wrap a clawlike hand around his right wrist, preventing him from jamming the blade into the vampire's back as he'd wanted to do. Romeo's left shoulder was pinned against the gate by Paris's other arm, so he was unable to swing at the vampire.

"How's this for proof?" the count hissed as his jaw hinged open. It was obvious that the vampire was preparing to bite Romeo in the neck.

Romeo trembled for a brief moment, fearful that the count was about to kill him. But he found the nerve to face his enemy in spite of it.

"You'll have to do more than that to convince me,"

he said, ramming his right knee into Count Paris's rib cage.

The vampire didn't falter much—just a short cough—but his concentration broke long enough for Romeo to bring his head back and crash it against Count Paris, striking him between his blazing red eyes.

Count Paris stumbled backward and gave Romeo a little space to move, but Romeo remained in the vampire's clutches. Paris twisted Romeo's right arm so hard, Romeo thought it was going to snap.

"I will do whatever it takes to kill you," the vampire said.

"Excellent, then I will live happily with Juliet in heaven," Romeo proclaimed, plowing his left fist into the count's temple.

Paris was stunned, but quickly regrouped and landed a swift, hard kick to Romeo's left leg, causing it to wobble beneath him. Then the count swiped at Romeo with a fierce, monstrous hand, which spliced open his opponent's cheek.

As streams of blood trickled down his shirt collar, Romeo thought this might be the end of him. Perhaps he should give up. Yes, he wanted to see Juliet's body before he died, but if the vampire killed him now, he would be spared the agony of holding his love in his arms for the very last time.

However, when Count Paris growled into his ear, "If Juliet let a wretched Montague defile her body, then it's probably best that she's dead," Romeo's will to fight was renewed.

With a ferocious yell, he shoved the count away from him with his left shoulder, whipping his wrist out of Paris's hand in one rapid movement. He thrust his dagger straight ahead, but the vampire dodged it with a nimble duck.

"Well, that certainly lit a fire under you," Count Paris said, laughing.

Romeo tried to catch him again, but Paris leaped up in the air like a vicious panther. When the vampire came down, he jammed his elbow straight into Romeo's collarbone, sending unbelievable pain through Romeo's arm and causing him to drop his dagger.

Romeo quickly bent down and tried to recover it, but the vampire planted his foot on the dagger and kicked it at least twenty feet away, under the wrought-iron gate and far out of Romeo's reach.

Count Paris rolled his neck back and forth, readying himself for his final assault. "Prepare to take your last breath, Montague!"

Romeo's eyes flitted about, looking for anything he could turn into a weapon. There was little around him, but behind Count Paris was an enormous tree with some low-hanging branches. Drenched in sweat and aching all over, Romeo didn't have time to consider a plan thoroughly. So when Count Paris came flying at him, he charged the vampire as well.

For a few seconds, everything slowed down in Romeo's mind. The count's pursuit seemed to freeze in time and he was able to exhale long enough to regain his strength. Then the world began to spin again and the vampire was speeding toward him.

At the last possible moment, Romeo dipped down to the dirt floor and slid underneath the count's legs.

The vampire spun around in the air as Romeo ran for the tree. Count Paris gave chase while Romeo reached up and hastily broke off a branch with his bare hands. As his pulse raced, Romeo snapped it over his knee and jutted the sharp, jagged edge of the wood directly in front of him. The lightning-fast Count Paris didn't see it coming. He flew at Romeo at full speed, the branch puncturing his chest and piercing his heart.

Romeo watched in relief as some of the life drained from the vampire's scarlet red eyes. But much to his surprise, Count Paris swiftly clamped his hands on Romeo's throat and squeezed.

"I'm n-not through with y-you yet," he stammered as he choked Romeo with his fingers.

Apparently Count Paris had not been exaggerating about his powers. He truly was one of the strongest vampires in Transylvania, if not the strongest of all. But as he gasped for air, Romeo realized that he had one last chance to defeat the count. He remembered that there were two vials in his trouser pockets—one that was filled with poison and another that was filled with holy water.

As he dug feverishly through both his pockets, Romeo's throat began to close up. Count Paris was putting every ounce of his depleting energy into tightening his grip on his neck. The two smooth vials slipped out of his fingers once, but he finally grabbed hold of the one in his right pocket. Romeo did not know which vial he had in his hand; however, he would find out as soon as he splashed the contents onto the vampire's face.

Coughing and wheezing, Romeo uncapped the vial and immediately poured every drop of the liquid onto Count Paris's head and body. The vampire instantly let go of him, screaming in absolute agony; then he fell on the ground, writhing around in pain.

Romeo shuddered in disgust when he saw clouds of smoke rising off of the count's skin. His flesh was burning right off of his bones. In less than a minute, the vampire was reduced to a pile of bloody pulp, and Romeo was finally victorious.

Rubbing his aching neck, Romeo surveyed the ground. He looked everywhere for a glint of a turquoise stone, and after only a few minutes of searching, he found it in a patch of dry grass. He picked the ring up, blew off the dirt, and rubbed it on his cloak until it shined.

Then, the smell of death billowing up into the evening sky, Romeo Montague went in search of his wife.

CHAPTER TWENTY

fter the funeral, Juliet had been laid on a flat slab of marble in the center of her tomb, with her hands folded neatly on her chest. She had been dressed in the gorgeous silk dupioni gown her nurse had laid out for her the night before her unconscious body had been found. The clergyman had closed her eyes shut before he began the proceedings, so all she could do now was hear.

And Juliet had heard plenty during her eulogy. More weeping from her inconsolable mother and nurse. Her father had cursed her soul more than once. But what was still ringing in Juliet's ears was the whispering from the other vampires who had come to her funeral to pay their respects.

"You have to admire the girl for sticking to her principles," one gentleman had said.

"I would have admired her more if she had married Count Paris," a woman had replied. "I doubt he will help us with Prince Radu now."

Juliet knew that the woman had spoken the truth. The count had been so upset by his future bride's suicide that he'd left before the funeral had concluded. But as much as it hurt to accept that her actions carried such great consequences for others, if Juliet was given the chance to repeat the last twenty-four hours, she would not change a thing. What she had done was done in the name of true love—none of the Capulets, not even her repentant mother, would ever understand.

Just then, the sound of footsteps created a large booming echo inside the crypt. Juliet knew that it was Romeo, coming to fetch her, just as Friar Laurence had promised. Oh, how she wished that she could move any part of her body. She would have given anything and everything to wake up from this trance and run to her husband. She couldn't bear being in this strange state much longer.

As the footsteps came closer, Juliet imagined what her life with Romeo would be like once the friar performed the purification process. She would be her true self again—a young, vibrant, happy woman, not a vampire. She would bear children with him and grow old with him. They would build a cottage with a stone chimney and have a flower garden, somewhere in the hills, far away from Transylvania. They would read to each other by the fireplace, and hold each other in bed as they drifted off to sleep. To Juliet, there was nothing more perfect and beautiful than this daydream, and as soon as the friar's potion wore off, it would become reality.

Any second now.

The sound of footsteps stopped just outside the tomb's entrance, and there was a long-drawn-out pause. Juliet's heart was pounding with anticipation. But then she was startled by a deep, distraught cry—one that she had hoped to hear emerge from her father's mouth, but never materialized, not even at the funeral.

Juliet's excitement turned to fright as the sobbing became louder. This could not be her Romeo. He would have been bouncing off the tomb's walls with happiness, knowing that they were only hours away from being free and together forever. Perhaps it was her father, finally coming to his senses and mourning his only child. However, once the crying subsided, the voice she had waited all night and day to hear whispered softly and tenderly, right into her ear.

"Juliet, my love. What have you done?"

It was Romeo, without a shred of doubt.

"Why would you not wait for me?"

Juliet's mind was flooded with an ocean of confused thoughts. All she had done was try to save herself, and she was waiting for him—just like the friar had instructed. Juliet tried to move her lips and respond to Romeo, but she was still paralyzed, from the tips of her toes to the crown of her head.

"Oh, God, I cannot take this any longer. My wife, my friend, my everything is dead," Romeo muttered.

Juliet let out a bloodcurdling scream, and yet there was nothing but silence. How could Romeo think she was actually dead? Did he not know of Friar Laurence's plan? Had there been some kind of misunderstanding? Juliet's dream was quickly turning into a nightmare from which she was desperate to awake.

The potion should be wearing off soon. She prayed over and over again that Romeo would stay here in the tomb until it did.

"Juliet, I made a vow to love you in all ways and for all seasons," Romeo professed, his voice drained of its natural light and luster. "Since you are no longer of this place and time, I will join you in the next realm."

These words of misery and hopelessness gave Juliet a new wave of panic. Inside, she was wailing and begging God to spare her husband. If she could open her eyes and mouth, everything would be fine. Then she felt it—a slight tingling sensation at the bottoms of her bare feet that was gradually traveling up her calves toward her knees.

"This world would never accept us. Our families would rather see us dead than married," Romeo said bitterly. "But in heaven, we will be what we should have been, and more. So now I sip this poisonous brew, and lie down and die right beside you."

The tingling sensation had moved through the upper half of her body, almost reaching her neck and head. Juliet willed every limb and sense of hers to come back to life. She had to get to Romeo before he reached the point of no return.

Juliet's hands were the first parts of her body to become mobile, then her arms. She reached down toward her belly and felt Romeo's head, lying there, still. She ran her fingers through his hair, hoping this would rouse him, but it did not. Her legs were given back their circulation, and soon after that, she could sit up somewhat.

Although every part of her ached all over, Juliet's heart hurt worst of all, especially when her eyes fluttered open and she saw Romeo slumped over her. There was a large cut on his face and an empty vial lying on the floor near his boots. Juliet had not regained her speech yet, so she shook Romeo as hard as she could. There was no response.

Juliet put her ear next to Romeo's lips—she could feel no air passing through them. Then she put her hand on top of his chest, which was no longer rising and falling. Once she realized just how bleak Romeo's fate was, her mouth hung open and out came the most calamitous and pitiful shriek. Tears poured out of her red eyes and down her white cheeks as her shoulders shook and head hung low. Finally, her voice had returned.

"Wake up, darling! Wake up, I am here," Juliet whimpered as she kissed Romeo on the back of his neck. "It is time to see the friar. He's going to make me human again."

However, with each moment that ebbed away without any movement from Romeo, Juliet lost hope that he would ever awaken or that she would return to Friar Laurence. For why would she want to live—as a human or vampire—in a place where her dearest, most precious love would never be with her?

"This is pure torture," Juliet moaned as she gently rolled Romeo off of her and placed him on the ground. "It hurts to talk or see or even breathe."

After running her hand down the side of his bloodstained cheek and the center of his chest, she frantically reached for the vial from which Romeo had taken his fatal sips.

"I could wait hours to starve, but I am not that strong," Juliet said to herself.

She dipped her head back and opened her mouth, tapping the vial above it with her fingers so that she could swallow a few drops. Unfortunately, the container was bone dry.

"God, whatever sin I am being punished for, please,

take me now and end my suffering!" Juliet shouted through another surge of tears.

There was no sign sent down from above, so Juliet leaned over her husband's body, laying her head down near his shoulder. She did not hear it at first, for the sound of her crying was reverberating throughout the cold tomb. But when she finally settled down, she was able to hear a faint rhythm coming from her beloved's heart.

This was an absolute miracle, but Juliet had no time to rejoice. There was only one way that she could save him, and that was to turn him into a bloodthirsty vampire. When she thought about doing this without Romeo's consent, she felt a throbbing ache in the center of her chest. But when she considered the alternative, the ache penetrated every part of her.

So Juliet closed her eyes and summoned a power that had been flowing through her body for days, a power that she had hoped she would never have to use. Juliet craned her neck back, feeling a hot spring of energy explode inside of her. With all of her strength, she pulled Romeo toward her, his head hanging back.

She inhaled deeply and opened her mouth. Two of her top and bottom teeth transformed into fangs. She brushed a lock of Romeo's hair away from his neck with her long fingernails and stared at a purple vein winding down from behind his ear toward his collarbone.

Then she leaned over, skimmed her lips against his skin, and dug her pointed teeth into his neck.

With each drop of Montague blood that she swallowed, Juliet could feel a larger, more significant transformation taking place inside of her. While she could sense that parts of her body were shutting down—including her heart—other parts, like her bones and muscles, were swelling with a type of kinetic energy that was completely indescribable. It made her feel like she could climb to the top of the highest peak in the Carpathian Mountains or swim across the ocean in a matter of minutes. She prayed that the same thing would happen to Romeo after all this was over.

Juliet knew that she had to pull back at some point, but when? No one had ever told her how to turn someone, so she would have to go with her instinct, although right now her instinct was pressuring her to ingest every bit of Romeo's blood. She watched her husband's complexion and how its color was fading away. She could also feel that his skin was icy cold when she touched it with her fingers. Using every ounce of restraint she could muster, she slowly let go of his neck.

"Romeo. Romeo," she murmured, gently kissing the two pink marks that her teeth had left on his skin. "Please come back to me."

Juliet stared at his face, willing his eyes to open or his lips to move. She repeatedly said his name, much like a magical incantation, and held him tight against her chest. But Romeo did not come back, not even for one brief, fleeting moment. There was no mistaking what had just transpired—all of Juliet's efforts had failed and Romeo was dead. She let out one last agonized cry.

The sound of rain pattering against the roof of the crypt slowly eased Juliet into a serene, almost catatonic state. Her mind was void of all thoughts, until one came into stark focus. She tenderly laid Romeo down on the floor of the tomb. She dug into his boot and took hold of his parrying dagger, then ascended and staggered toward a wooden sculpture of Vlad the Impaler, holding up the severed head of a Montague by the hair.

"This is thy sheath," she said plainly.

Juliet steadied her trembling hands and stabbed the dagger directly into Vladimir's chest, chipping away at the wood and sending a few jagged shards fluttering to the ground. Juliet got down on her knees and sifted through the wood, looking for the largest, longest, sturdiest piece she could find. Once she found one that was of the desired size, she ran the serrated edge across the palm of her hand to see if it would be sharp enough to penetrate both her ribs and her heart. It was so sharp that it scratched her skin deep enough to draw blood.

Juliet winced a little, but forged ahead, her soul in far worse anguish than any kind of physical pain a person could ever endure. She crawled over to Romeo's body and sat next to him, kissing his forehead as though they were just beginning an ordinary night's sleep. Then she pointed the tip of the shard at her heart, closed her eyes for the last time, and said, "Let me die."

But before she could plunge the self-made wooden stake into her chest, a quaking hand grabbed one of her wrists. The instant she felt it, Juliet let go of the shard, one finger at a time, until the object fell out of her grasp. When she opened her eyes, they were met by Romeo's, which were loving and alive and shining like red crystal.

Juliet gasped—elated that Romeo had not died—but then she realized that for him to fully transform, he had to drink some of her blood. She was so relieved to have remembered this step—she would certainly have lost Romeo forever otherwise. Juliet held her bloody palm to his mouth and said, "Drink, my love, please."

Romeo nodded and sipped Juliet's blood out of her cupped hand. Within moments, the wounds on his face slowly began to vanish and his skin turned the palest shade of white.

Realizing that she had brought him back from the brink of death, Juliet laughed in relief and crumbled on top of him so her cheek pressed against his chest. He wrapped his arms around her and caressed her back with his still-quivering hands.

"I thought you had left me," he whispered.

"It is a long story, but I was under the spell of a powerful potion," Juliet responded, her voice cracking with joy and agony in every word she spoke. "Friar Laurence was supposed to have sent a messenger to you."

Romeo stroked Juliet's hair delicately, as though it were spun from gold. "Moldova has been quarantined. Smallpox outbreak. The messenger must not have made it past the border."

Juliet placed her hand on her chest and realized that her heart was no longer beating—and it never would again. With a quarantine in place, the friar would never be able to reach the shaman in Moldova. The window of time they had to perform the purification process would close before they could devise another plan—Tybalt's corpse would soon be unusable and who knew when another dead vampire would turn up? If Lord Capulet was successful in getting Prince Radu to revoke the peace treaty, then that could be never.

She and Romeo would remain vampires forever. But as she gazed upon her loving husband, Juliet thought perhaps that might not be the worst thing in the world.

"I might not have made it either, if it had not been for you," Romeo said, touching Juliet's chin. "I owe you my thanks."

"You do not owe me that," Juliet said, taking his hand in hers. "Because of me, we are now both sentenced to a life of everlasting depravity."

Romeo pulled Juliet up by the arms so that their foreheads were pressed together. She tilted her head when he'd tilted his, and she leaned toward him as they closed their eyes. She felt the tenderness of his lips trace the outline of her cheekbones.

Then he gripped her tightly and said, "All that matters is that we're together."

Unlike Tybalt, who had told her just the other day that his capacity to feel was compromised when he became a vampire, Juliet was met with startling waves of emotion crashing all around her. Romeo ran his fingers through her soft hair, his thumb grazing her forehead. She tipped her head slightly, her gaze steadily trained on his face. He leaned closer to her, then closer still. When Juliet felt his soft, inviting lips press gently against hers, she surrendered to that wondrous current, letting it carry her toward the horizon, where the sun never shone and this beautiful kiss lasted until the end of time.

EPILOGUE

That night, Romeo and Juliet fled Transylvania together, with only the clothes on their backs. They made their way through the Carpathian Mountains and crossed the northwestern border into Hungary. Eventually, the couple settled in the far outskirts of the country. They built a modest stone home in a beautiful, open meadow with greenery and a babbling brook. They lived there happily and peacefully for many years, consuming only the blood of the animals that they hunted by the light of the moon.

As they aged, Juliet was afraid that their bodies would begin to weaken, much like the bodies of her parents, which she tried to track down after she'd gone to the castle one day and saw that it had been abandoned. Romeo, however, believed that true love and their pure (but dead) hearts had saved them from withering away. Once they brought a child into the world—a beautiful boy, who they named Laurence— Juliet could finally admit that Romeo might be right.

EDITOR'S NOTE

The rest of the vampires had no choice but to leave Transylvania, too. Lord and Lady Capulet were unable to convince Prince Radu to revoke, or even amend, his peace treaty. Then what they had feared became a reality—the vulnerable Capulets were forced to give up their castle and riches as reparations to the families of all those who had been killed during Vladimir's reign. Suddenly faced with immortal but weakened bodies, and their new status as commoners, the Capulets disbanded, pairing off and fleeing to various sections of Bulgaria, Bosnia, and Albania.

Some of the vampires lived like wild beasts—invading villages and preying on innocents one after the other, then moving to another town once the food supply thinned out. Some of them longed to return to civilized society so they found a way to hide their true vampire identities. These cunning creatures resided among the living, worked with them in town, and dined with them at parties. They would use their wit, intelligence, and charm to cast a potent spell on the most impressionable of humans, then gain their trust—and oftentimes, their love.

As time went on, some of these secret vampires became assimilated and refused to kill like their brothers and sisters in arms. Instead, these enlightened vampires would reveal themselves and appeal to the mercy of their human counterparts. In many cases, the vampires had little trouble convincing them to be turned. It was no surprise that humans suffered from vanity and fear of death, so they were willing to earn immortality and offer their blood as the ultimate sacrifice without truly knowing what they were getting themselves into.

Historians believe that the Vampire Diaspora is what caused the proliferation of the species over the centuries. By the mid-1600s, descendants of the Capulets were scattered throughout Europe—France, Sweden, Norway, Poland, Italy, and Portugal, to name a few of the countries to which they emigrated. By the late 1800s, the vampire population in England, Scotland, Ireland, and all of North America had grown at an alarming rate.

Today, vampires have a worldwide presence, and in some cases, they live among us openly. As for the other cases, they are most likely hiding in the shadows and waiting patiently, for just the right moment to turn us . . .

   . . . into them.

WILLIAM SHAKESPEARE was born in Stratford-upon-Avon, England, in 1564. He is widely regarded as the greatest writer in the English language. His body of work consists of thirty-eight plays and more than one hundred and fifty sonnets, as well as other poetry. We're pretty sure he would think this version of his play is awesome.

CLAUDIA GABEL grew up in Binghamton, New York, and dreamed of being a writer. Now she is the author of the In or Out series for teens, which means she has extensive knowledge of deadly drama, enemies, and feuding. Shakespeare would be proud.

For exclusive information
on your favorite authors and artists,
visit www.authortracker.com.

Read on for an excerpt from

LITTLE *Vampire* WOMEN

Chapter One

PLAYING PILGRIMS

"Christmas won't be Christmas without any corpses," grumbled Jo, lying on the rug.

"It's so dreadful to be poor!" sighed Meg, looking down at her old dress.

"I don't think it's fair for some vampires to have plenty of pretty squirming things, and other vampires nothing at all," added little Amy, with an injured sniff.

Being so poor, the Marches customarily dined on quarts of pig's blood, goat's blood, and, on very special occasions, cow's blood, but they rarely had the luxury of a living, breathing animal to feast on, and when they did, it was usually a small creature hardly more than a snack. Most of their meals had to be warmed over the fire to be brought up to the proper temperature, which was particularly humiliating for the four March girls. Some were the days when they could sink their fangs into a wiggling beaver, let alone a writhing cow. A human had never been on the menu, even when the family was wealthy and lived in a large, well-appointed house, for the Marches were humanitarians who believed the consumption of humans unworthy of the modern vampire. Humans were an inferior species in many ways, but they deserved to be pitied, not consumed.

"We've got Father and Mother, and each other," said Beth contentedly from her corner. She was the shy, domestically inclined sister.

"We haven't got Father, and shall not have him for a long time," Jo said sadly. She didn't say "perhaps never," but each silently added it, thinking of Father far away, where the fighting was.

The war was the reason they were to be denied even a field mouse this Christmas. It was going to be a hard winter for all humans, and their mother thought they ought not spend money for pleasure, when so many were suffering in the army. That the suffering was limited to mortal men did not concern Mother, for her commitment to the human race was steadfast, despite the criticism of her neighbors, who found both the Marches' beliefs and behavior baffling. Typically, vampires didn't concern themselves with the petty wars of humans. They had roamed the earth long before people and would continue to roam it long after they were gone.

"We can't do much, but we can make our little

sacrifices, and ought to do it gladly. But I am afraid I don't," and Meg shook her head, as she thought regretfully of all the pretty corpses she wouldn't get to eat.

"But I don't think the little we should spend would do any good. We've each got a dollar, and the army wouldn't be much helped by our giving that. I agree not to expect any gifts from Mother or you, but I do want to buy *Mr. Bloody Wobblestone's Scientific Method for Tracking, Catching, and Destroying Vampire Slayers.*[1] I've wanted it so long," said Jo, who yearned to join the league of defenders, brave and gallant vampires who protected their fellow creatures from those humans who would destroy them by any means possible. In the last century, the noble profession had undergone a vast change, adopting modern techniques to battle an ancient threat. Relying on one's instincts, which had always been an imperfect process at best and a guessing game at worst, had been supplanted by steadfast science. Now, instead of spending three months learning the antiquated art of filtering out the smothering scent of garlic, one simply could put on an allium mask,[2] which accomplished the task for you.

---

[1] Bestselling how-to that introduced the so-called scientifical method of slayer hunting, by Clifford Farmer (b. 1685).

[2] Invented by Willis Whipetten (1750–1954) for his son, John, who suffered from dysgeusia garlisima, a chemosensory disorder that makes everything smell like garlic.

"I planned to spend my dollar in new music," said Beth, who loved to play music on the Marches' very old, poorly tuned piano. Mrs. March believed in a liberal education and strove to cultivate an interest in the arts in all her children.

"I shall get a nice box of Faber's fang enhancements," said Amy decidedly. Her fangs, though long, were blunt and did not come to an aristocratic point like her sisters'. No one minded the dullness save herself, but Amy felt deeply the want of a pair of killer-looking fangs.

"Mother didn't say anything about our money, and she won't wish us to give up everything. Let's each buy what we want, and have a little fun; I'm sure we work hard enough to earn it," cried Jo.

"I know I do—teaching those tiresome children nearly all night, when I'm longing to enjoy myself at home," began Meg, in the complaining tone again.

"You don't have half such a hard time as I do," said Jo, who served as companion and protector to their 427-year-old aunt. "How would you like to be shut up for hours with a nervous, fussy old lady who's convinced every tradesman who comes to the door is there to slay her?"

"It's naughty to fret, but I do think washing dishes and keeping things tidy is the worst work in the world. It makes me cross," Beth said.

"I don't believe any of you suffer as I do," cried Amy,

"for you don't have to go to school with impertinent girls who plague you if you don't know your lessons, and laugh at your dresses, and label your father if he isn't rich, and insult you when your fangs aren't nice."

"If you mean libel, I'd say so, and not talk about labels, as if Papa was a pickle bottle," advised Jo, laughing.

As young readers like to know "how people look," we will take this moment to give them a little sketch of the four sisters, who sat knitting away in the near dawn, while the December snow fell quietly without, and the fire crackled cheerfully within. It was a comfortable room, though the carpet was faded and the furniture very plain, for a good picture or two hung on the walls, books filled the recesses, chrysanthemums and Christmas roses bloomed in the windows, and a pleasant atmosphere of home peace pervaded it.

Margaret, the eldest of the four, looked to be about sixteen, and very pretty, being plump and fair, with large eyes, plenty of soft brown hair, a sweet mouth, and white hands, of which she was rather vain. A year younger, Jo was very tall, thin, and brown, and reminded one of a colt, for she never seemed to know what to do with her long limbs, which were very much in her way. She had a decided mouth, a comical nose, and sharp, gray eyes, which appeared to see everything and were by turns fierce, funny, or thoughtful. Her long, thick hair was her one beauty, but it was usually bundled into a net, to be out of her way. Round shoulders had Jo, big hands and feet, a flyaway look to her clothes, and the uncomfortable appearance of a girl who was rapidly shooting up into a woman and didn't like it. (Although her transformation to vampire brought an abrupt end to the growth spurt, the awkwardness of her appearance remained a permanent fixture.) Elizabeth, or Beth, as everyone called her, appeared to be an ashen-faced, smooth-haired, bright-eyed girl of thirteen, with a shy manner, a timid voice, and a peaceful expression which was seldom disturbed. Her father called her "Little Miss Tranquility," and the name suited her excellently, for she seemed to live in a happy world of her own, only venturing out to meet the few whom she trusted and loved. Amy, though the youngest, was a most important person, in her own opinion at least. A regular snow maiden, with blue eyes, and yellow hair curling on her shoulders, pale and slender, and always carrying herself like a young vampire lady mindful of her manners.

Each girl looked as if she'd been alive for scarcely more than a decade, especially Amy, whose pallid complexion could do little to mute her youthful energy, but they had all undergone the Great Change thirty-two years previous, which made them vampires of some experience. However, they were still considered adolescents, for vampires lived very long lives indeed and thirty-odd years was scarcely a fraction of it. Therefore, in all the ways that mattered, the March girls, although chronologically older than their mortal counterparts, were perched just as precariously on the edge of womanhood.

The clock struck six. Mother was coming, and everyone brightened to welcome her.

"I'll tell you what we should do," said Beth, "let's each get Marmee something for Christmas, and not get anything for ourselves."

"That's like you, dear! What will we get?" exclaimed Jo.

Everyone thought soberly for a minute, then Meg announced, "I shall get her a rabbit to feed on."

"A squirrel," cried Jo.

"A bunny," said Beth.

"I'll get a little mouse. It won't cost much, so I'll have some left to buy my fang enhancements," added Amy.

"How will we give the things?" asked Meg.

"Put them on the table, and bring her in and see her open the bundles. Don't you remember how we used to do on our birthdays?" answered Jo.

Having decided how to present their gifts, the girls discussed where to buy them, for the only store on Main Street that sold small animals was a pet shop and they didn't know how Mr. Lewis would feel about providing tasty delicacies for their mother. Concord was an integrated town, where vampires could live peacefully in the open, but there were still moments when

7

reminders of a vampire's particular lifestyle could make the locals uncomfortable.

Though they were eager to buy presents, they had to stay indoors, for the sun was about to rise. Jo suggested they practice hunting vampire slayers, her favorite occupation, and the girls complied reluctantly, for they didn't share Jo's passion. Meg was the slayer and Jo tracked her to the attic closet, where her quarry had already chopped the heads off Beth's poor, blameless doll. Beth protested the unfair abuse and attached a neat little cap to the poor invalid's neck. As both arms and legs had been removed during a previous field exercise, she had to wrap the deformed doll in a blanket.

Her sisters laughed at the makeshift hospital ward she assembled.

"Glad to find you so merry, my girls," said a cheery voice at the door, and the girls turned to welcome a tall, motherly lady with a "can I help you" look about her which was truly delightful. She was not elegantly dressed, but a noble-looking woman of forty biological years, and the girls thought the gray cloak and unfashionable bonnet covered the most splendid mother in the world.

"Well, dearies, how have you got on tonight? There was so much to do that I didn't come home to dinner. Has anyone called, Beth? How is your cold, Meg? Jo, you look tired to death. Come and kiss me, baby."

While making these maternal inquiries, Mrs. March took off her artificial teeth to reveal her well-appointed fangs. Some vampire ladies in the community thought it was just the thing to walk around with their teeth hanging out, but Marmee thought naked fangs were an indecency on par with naked ankles.

As they gathered about the table, Mrs. March said, with a particularly happy face, her fangs gleaming white in the firelight, "I've got a treat for you."

A quick, bright smile went round like a streak of moonshine. Beth clapped her hands, and Jo cried, "A letter! A letter! Three cheers for Father!"

"Yes, a nice long letter. He is well, and thinks he shall get through the cold season better than we feared. He sends all sorts of loving wishes for Christmas, and an especial message to you girls," said Mrs. March.

"I think it was so splendid of Father to go at all when the war has nothing to do with vampires," said Meg warmly.

The War Between the States was over the moral issue of slavery, which was indeed of little interest to vampires. However, slave quarters were verdant feeding grounds for vampires south of the Mason-Dixon Line, for their inhabitants were often too tired from days of backbreaking, abusive labor to put up a fight, and the slaves who disappeared were often mistakenly assumed to have fled north with the help of abolitionists. Being an ethical vampire with implacable morals,

Mr. March felt he should do his part to help win the war his kind had unintentionally started by making it seem as though the North was interfering extensively in private Southern business.

"Don't I wish I could go as a drummer, a vivan—what's its name? Or a nurse, so I could be near him and help him," exclaimed Jo, who would rather do anything than work for her awful aunt March.

"When will he come home, Marmee?" asked Beth, with a little quiver in her voice.

"Not for many months, dear. He will stay and do his work faithfully as long as he can, and we won't ask for him back a minute sooner than he can be spared. Now come and hear the letter."

They all drew to the fire, Mother in the big chair with Beth at her feet, Meg and Amy perched on either arm of the chair, and Jo leaning on the back, where no one would see any sign of emotion if the letter should happen to be touching.

Very few human letters were written in those hard times that were not touching, especially those which fathers sent home, and this vampire letter was no different. In it little was said of the hardships endured, the dangers faced, or the homesickness conquered. It was a cheerful, hopeful letter, full of the comical lengths Mr. March often had to go to in order to avoid sunshine. He'd joined the army as a chaplain and tried very hard to stay inside his tent during daylight hours, but this was not always practical, as war followed no schedule. Only at the end did the writer's heart overflow with fatherly love and longing for the little vampire girls at home.

"Give them all of my dear love and a kiss. Tell them I think of them by night, pray for them by day, and find my best comfort in their affection at all times. A year seems very long to wait before I see them, but remind them that while we wait we may all work, so that these hard days need not be wasted. I know they will remember all I said to them, that they will be loving children to you, will do their duty faithfully and fight their bosom enemy bravely," he said, referring to the demon beast that lived inside them all. It was a daily challenge to overcome their vampire natures, but Mr. March knew his girls could do it and from afar he urged them to "conquer themselves so beautifully that when I come back to them I may be fonder and prouder than ever of my little vampire women." Everybody sniffed when they came to that part. Jo wasn't ashamed of the great bloody tear[3] that dropped off the end of her nose and landed in a bright red splatter on her otherwise pristine dress, and Amy never minded the rumpling of her

---

[3] Paulson Dillywither (1834–1897) argues convincingly in *Vampire Habits and Customs: The Beastly True Nature of Nature's True Beast* that lacrimal hemoglobin emissions, also known as blood tears, are caused by an infiltration of blood into the nasolacrimal duct.

curls as she hid her face on her mother's shoulder and sobbed out, "I am a selfish girl! But I'll truly try to be better, so he mayn't be disappointed in me by-and-by."

"We all will," cried Meg. "I think too much of drinking cow and deer blood and wearing beautiful silk gloves, but I won't anymore, if I can help it."

"I'll try and be what he loves to call me, 'a little vampire woman,' and not be rough and wild, but do my duty here instead of wanting to be somewhere else," said Jo, thinking that keeping her temper at home was a much harder task than facing a rebel or two down South.

Beth said nothing, but wiped away tears with the blue army sock and began to knit with all her might, losing no time in doing the duty that lay nearest her, while she resolved in her quiet little soul to be all that Father hoped to find her when the year brought round the happy coming home.

Mrs. March broke the silence that followed Jo's words, by saying in her cheery voice, "Do you remember how you used to play *Vilgrim's Progress*[4] when you were young things? Nothing delighted you more than

---

[4] Seminal text that first suggested vampires were children of God and therefore worthy of entrance into heaven; by William Swinton (1321–1569). Swinton cited the gift of immortality as proof of God's preference for vampires over their mortal counterparts and even hinted that humanity itself might be damned. John Bunyan's *The Pilgrim's Progress* is largely thought to be an almost verbatim rip-off of the book, although defenders have argued it is a pastiche.

to have me tie my piece bags on your backs for burdens, give you hats and sticks and rolls of paper, and let you travel through the house from the cellar, which was the City of Destruction, up, up, to the housetop, where you had all the lovely things you could collect to make a Celestial City."

"What fun it was, especially going by the lions, fighting Apollyon, and passing through the valley where the hobgoblins were," said Jo, for all the challenges that poor Vilgrim, the vampire pilgrim, had to overcome in his quest for heaven greatly resembled a course for the training of vampire defenders.

"I liked the place where the bundles fell off and tumbled downstairs," said Meg.

"I don't remember much about it, except that I was afraid of the sunlight that poured into the attic. If I wasn't too old for such things, I'd rather like to play it over again," said Amy, who really was too old for childish games despite her persistently youthful appearance.

"We never are too old for this, my dear, because it is a play we are playing all the time in one way or another. Our burdens are here, our road is before us, and the longing for goodness is the guide that leads us through many troubles, mistakes, and uncontrollable feeding frenzies to inner peace which is the true Celestial City. Now, my little vilgrims, suppose you begin again, not in play, but in earnest, and see how far on you can get before Father comes home," Marmee suggested, concerned now, as always, with the preservation of her daughters' souls, for it had not been that many years past since vampires were thought to have no soul at all. For centuries, they were considered minions of the devil and were forced to hide in shadow, fearful that any seemingly harmless gathering of people would quickly become an angry, stake-bearing mob. But thanks to the Camp Moldovenească Accords[5] that was all in the past.

"Really, Mother? Where are our bundles?" asked Amy, who was a very literal vampire.

"Each of you told what your burden was just now, except Beth. I rather think she hasn't got any," said her mother.

"Yes, I have. Mine is dishes and dusters, and envying vampires with nice pianos, and being afraid of people."

---

[5] The international meeting held in 1767 that officially established vampires as naturalized citizens of heaven and granted them full inalienable rights. Out of the Accords came the groundbreaking Swift Nourishment Act, which reclassified the vampiric method of attaining sustenance as commerce, thereby making the consumption of humans who fell below the poverty level a safe and legal option for hungry vampires, as long as said vampires met the asking price and filled out the appropriate paperwork. Named for Jonathan Swift, who first proposed the arrangement in his famous 1729 essay "A Modest Proposal," in which he recommended that Ireland's poor solve their economic woes by selling their children for food.

Beth's bundle was such a funny one that everybody wanted to laugh, but nobody did, for it would have hurt her feelings very much.

"Let us do it," said Meg thoughtfully. "It is only another name for trying to be good, and the story may help us, for though we don't want to feed on humans, it's hard work resisting our basic demon natures."

They talked over the new plan while old Hannah cleared the table, then out came the four little work baskets, and the needles flew as the girls made black-out curtains for Aunt March, who didn't trust the store-bought article to keep out the light. At nine, they stopped work and went to their coffins.